YETI OR KNOT

CASSANDRA ELIZZABETH

Kissing Camels Publishing LLC
1002 Lititz Pike #123
Lititz, PA 17543
First published in the United States September 2025

This is a work of fiction. Names, characters, places, and incidents either are the product of the author's imagination or are used fictitiously. Any resemblance to actual persons, living or dead, events, or locales is entirely coincidental.

ISBN 979-8-9895228-6-6

Formatting by EmCat Designs
Cover design by Fallnskye Illustration
Paperback formatting by EmCat Designs
Edited by Beth at Beth Hudson, Ink.
Proofed by Amanda at Beth Hudson, Ink.
PA Services provided by Amanda at Beth Hudson, Ink.

www.cassandraelizzabeth.com

DEDICATION

For all the girlies who'd let the cinnamon roll Yeti hit it.
No judgment. Just extra icing.

AUTHOR'S NOTE

When I was twenty-one, I went on the adventure of a lifetime—including an out-of-body experience in a small temple in Varanasi, trekking through a Himalayan mountain town that still lives in my soul. I came home, dreaming in Hindi, but a piece of me has always remained there, sipping chai on the ghats of the Ganges river.

So when I sat down to write a Yeti romance, I knew exactly where I wanted to return. This story gave me the excuse to not only revisit that incredible time in my life, but to imagine what might happen if something ancient and beautiful was waiting in the dark to claim me and keep me there forever.

Yeti or Knot is a spicy, emotional, and wildly devoted monster romance. It's filthy and tender in equal measure—a story for anyone who's ever wanted to be worshipped exactly as they are... even if it's by an eight-foot Yeti. (Or maybe especially if it's by an eight-foot Yeti.)

This story contains graphic sexual content (with the Yeti), including: knotting, primal play, sensory deprivation, size difference, squirting, ass play, just the tip, and breeding kink. You'll also find one cave (instead of one bed), accidental mating, a cinnamon roll monster, on page violence, and one unhinged cheating ex. There are also references to loss of a parent and genetic disease.

If monster romance, fated mates, exes getting what they deserve, and women in STEM getting absolutely wrecked by gentle giants is your thing—you're in the right cave.

Pour yourself a cup of chai and get lost in the frost with me.

Yeti or Knot, let's do this.

—*Cassandra*

CONTENT WARNINGS

- Betrayal and cheating (FMC's fiancé)
- Intimate partner violence (wrist-grabbing/controlling behavior by fiancé)
- Violence and peril in survival settings
- Mentions of death and loss
- Gore (animal attacks, blood)
- Kidnapping/forced proximity elements
- Explicit sexual content, including human/monster intimacy
- Size and power imbalance (consensual)
- Possessive/protective love interest
- Alcohol mention/use
- Terminal genetic disease

PLAYLIST

Breathe Me — Sia
Blood in the Cut — K. Flay
Ends of the Earth — Lord Huron
Shake It Out — Florence + The Machine
Out in the Open — Puggy, Rochelle Riser
Back That Azz Up — Juvenile
Every Breath You Take — Denmark + Winter
Wicked Game — Ursine Vulpine & Annaca
Home (Slowed) — Edith Whiskers
Wolf & I — Oh Land
Runaway — AURORA
Crazy in Love (feat. Wulf) — J2
Two Men in Love — The Irrepressibles
There's a Hero in You — Tommee Profitt
Rise Up — Andra Day
Stand By Me — Denmark + Winter
I Get to Love You — Ruelle

CHAPTER ONE

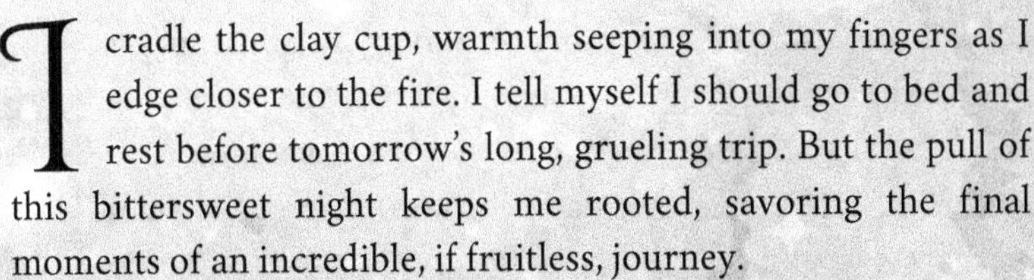

I cradle the clay cup, warmth seeping into my fingers as I edge closer to the fire. I tell myself I should go to bed and rest before tomorrow's long, grueling trip. But the pull of this bittersweet night keeps me rooted, savoring the final moments of an incredible, if fruitless, journey.

I take the final sip of my chai—the rich, creamy drink that is the essence of this place—its flavor lingering on my tongue as I half-listen to the other travelers swapping tales. Their voices melt into the background as my gaze drifts toward the woods across the Migaia river.

Moonlight pools like silver on the water, dappling trees in sharp relief against the night. Below the canopy, the forest floor vanishes into inky shadows, breathing secrets.

I don't know why I can't look away. I've seen this same view every night since I arrived, but tonight, something's alive in the air, crackling over my skin like electricity. I scan the riverbank, searching for the source until…there.

Two luminous eyes lock onto mine, glittering under the moonlight like the icy blue heart of Migshira, the holy glacier at the headwaters of this river. Too high for any local animal. Higher than a man's gaze would reach. Too large, too fierce and knowing to belong to the monkeys that call the trees home. Their gleam cuts through the dark with an intensity that steals my breath.

Who, or what, is watching me from the shadows?

A thrill courses through me, sharp and jagged, mingling fear with something darker. Hotter. My instincts scream at me to run, but my body won't move.

It's not just fear keeping me rooted; there's a pull in those eyes. A wordless promise of danger. And something else. Something primal and fierce I want to chase me down, and as crazy as it sounds, claim me.

Adrift in a sea of loss from my failed expedition and an uncertain future without the plant I so desperately need, the idea of belonging to something calls to my soul. An anchor.

I blink hard. When I open my eyes, the ones that were watching me are gone. Or maybe they were never there to begin with. My mind must be playing tricks on me. Exhaustion, or perhaps desperation.

The past few days were brutal as I pushed myself to find the *Silene vitalis*—the tiny, elusive flower that could save lives. Including my own.

A sudden snap of the fire pulls me from my thoughts. The travelers come back into focus, their laughter rising like sparks into the night. For a moment, I let the cozy scene wash over me, until a question cuts through.

"Have you ever seen one?" someone asks.

"Seen what?" My voice is steady, even as my pulse thrums beneath my skin as if those eyes were still sliding over me.

"A Migoi," the man replies, voice dropping low, as if one might be just beyond the ring of firelight. "They say their eyes catch the light, like stars in the night. Sometimes, if you're lucky, or unlucky, you might spot them watching."

Another traveler scoffs, waving the comment away, but the words claw their way into my mind. The locals spoke of such creatures, what I'd call a Yeti, with quiet reverence. I'd dismissed it as folklore woven from the mystique of these mountains.

But as an ethnobotanist, I've built my life around the places where science and stories intersect. It's not just the flora I study, but how people turn it into something sacred: meals, ceremonies, medicine, or maybe, just maybe, even the cure I need.

Now I can't help but wonder if the guardians of the mountains and forests might exist. After all, myths often hide a kernel of truth.

The man beside me claps a hand on my shoulder, jolting me from my thoughts. My face must've given me away—again.

"Don't let those guys spook you," he chuckles. "I've traveled all around the world and every culture has tales of watchers. But I've yet to see one myself."

I force a laugh, but my pulse keeps pounding. The others barely notice as I stand and say goodnight, the shadows pushing me toward the safety of my room.

Beyond the fire's glow, the cold bites harder, and the darkness presses close, heavy on my shoulders. I quicken my steps, the memory of those luminous eyes haunting me—piercing and inescapable.

What was it someone had said? *"Eyes like stars in the dark?"* That image gnaws at me. Could there really be Migoi in these mountains, watching from the forest beyond the river?

A rustle to my right snaps my nerves taut, every instinct screaming *move.* I realize how foolish I'd been, romanticizing the idea of something chasing me. Out here, alone in the dark, it feels less erotic, and far more terrifying.

Another sharp noise breaks the quiet, and I break into a run. I don't dare look back. By the time I reach my door, my hands are shaking, the key slipping against the lock. After a few tries, I get it open and slam the door shut behind me, breathing hard.

From the safety of my locked room, a nervous giggle escapes. I roll my eyes at my own foolishness of letting myself get spooked by a fireside tale.

The thick quilt on the bed promises comfort, its weight a soothing barrier against whatever lies outside. But even after I climb under it, unease clings to me—the eyes, the pull, the dark promise. Was it just exhaustion?

Three months of chasing that flower. Three months away from home. Away from Ben.

I wonder if he'll be as disappointed as I am. Or worse, what if he's not? But he loves me. Of course he will be just as upset as I am.

This foreboding must be the lingering thought of those damn eyes. But even if something is out there, it's not like it can follow me home tomorrow and I doubt I'll be back here anytime soon, if ever.

With my heart pounding like the death knell that awaits me without the damned *Silene vitalis,* sleep claims me.

The next morning, I make my way down the mountain, leaving behind the crisp, clean air of the Himalayas for the congested chaos of the city. At the airport, I tuck myself into a corner near my gate and type a quick message to Ben.

My thumbs hover over the phone. There's so much I'm not

saying. We didn't talk much while I was away, but I blamed it on time zones and packed schedules. Instead of hitting send, I lock the home screen. I'll be home soon, and we'll have time then to reconnect.

I open my laptop, thinking I might work, but the blank screen mocks me. Without the plant, there's nothing to do. Disappointment can wait until later.

Sighing, I stow the computer and scroll through photos on my phone instead. Smiling as faces and landscapes flick by: Sita, my guide-turned-friend, laughing; her father, Tenzig, ever the gracious host; the jagged peaks of the Himalayas piercing endless blue sky; and, of course, the plants.

I love India. The warmth of the people. The spicy food. The chai in clay cups. Somehow this vibrant land felt more like home than I expected. But reality is calling now. And more than anything, I miss Ben.

We've been so focused on our careers that we promised to prioritize us when I got back. Ben's has taken off while I stayed in the background. He landed a tenure-track position in our shared department of botany. I helped him grade papers, plan lessons—supporting him so we could build something together. By mutual agreement, we pushed his career first.

Now it's my turn. But I'm not sure how my failure will affect my degree or my future. Disappointment burns in my throat, along with the now-familiar tightening in my chest.

I'm older than most other doctoral candidates. Supporting Ben was a choice made with love, but I can't help wondering if I gambled too much?

No. We followed our plan. He's brilliant. Together, we'll figure this out. I just need to get home to him, back to our little house near the university, and everything will be okay.

When boarding is announced, I close the pictures and this chapter of my life. A grand adventure before settling into marriage.

But as I join the others in the boarding line, that hollow ache lingers. A whisper of everything I've left undiscovered—not just the plant, but also those damn silver eyes.

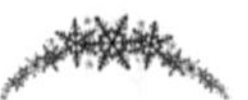

THE HOURS OF TRAVEL, customs, and jostling baggage claims leave me jetlagged, but as the taxi pulls up in front of my house, a tired smile curls my lips. Home sweet home.

I was disappointed when Ben texted me a few weeks ago he wouldn't be able to pick me up at the airport. But I understood how busy he was, and after all, what's one more hour after months apart?

Surprised to find the door locked, I frown. I imagined him throwing it open, sweeping me into his arms. We'd kiss our way to the shower, shedding our clothes until we were skin to skin again. Or at least that was my romanticized dream.

"Hello?" I call, stepping inside. No answer.

He knew I was coming home today. At least I think he did. The international date line always screws me up.

I kick off my shoes and shrug out of my jacket as I walk. The sound of running water makes me smile. He must be in the shower already, just as eager as I am to be together again.

I pause at the faint murmur of voices but dismiss it as one of the podcasts he always listens to. Stripping out of my travel-wrinkled clothes, I grab my robe and open the door to the bathroom. Just as I'm about to pull back the curtain and surprise him, a voice cuts through the steam.

"Oh, fuck yeah, just like that," Ben moans.

My stomach drops. That's no podcast. I back away, robe in hand, my mind casting for any possibility other than I didn't just come home to find Ben cheating on me. I jerk the robe on and frantically search the bedroom for proof that I'm wrong.

The photos of us on the dresser are gone. The slippers beside the bed aren't mine. I cross to his side and glance into the trash to find condom wrappers. I didn't want to be right, but here we are. The irrefutable evidence is staring me in the face.

Rage hits as fast and furious as the monsoon rains. I storm to the kitchen, grab the cleaning bucket from under the sink, and fill it with nugget ice from the machine he had to have, then top it off with cold water.

Balancing the bucket, I head back down the hall. Steam billows out from the bathroom, carrying the sound of a woman's voice.

I'm exhausted from traveling, in desperate need of a shower, and heartbroken from both my failed research expedition and being blindsided by Ben's cheating. But her breathy moan gives me the energy to climb up on the toilet, and lift the heavy bucket up as high as I can at the edge of the shower curtain.

I hear him again, the spicy words I had always wanted him to use with me spilling from his cheating lips for another. Betrayal pulses through me, sharp and raw, urging my arms up high enough to dump the whole damn thing over their heads.

The shriek from the mystery woman and the bellow from Ben of, "What the fuck!" brings a maniacal giggle from my lips. He rips back the curtain to reveal a woman kneeling at his feet with his now limp dick in her hand.

The empty bucket clatters to the floor and I say, "You're right, that nugget ice is where it's at."

CHAPTER TWO

"Jesus, Dahlia. I thought you were coming home tomorrow," he sputters as he pushes his hair out of his eyes.

And there it is. My failure to understand dates and times serendipitously saved me.

"Yeah, that pesky international date line is totally to blame for you putting your dick in someone else's mouth. Did you trip over it and fall?"

My eyes drift to the younger woman, and I snort. "Really, Ben? Is she your TA or your student? Could you be any more cliché? Get the fuck out, you worthless piece of shit."

"I'm not leaving. This is my house, too," he snaps.

I whip my phone off the counter where I'd left it and snap a picture of them. "Ben, I just flew halfway around the world. I am one second away from sending this to the dean and destroying you. Get. The. Fuck. Out."

He steps out, grabbing his robe off the back of the door and jerking it on. The younger woman, who looks vaguely familiar, whips her head back and forth between us like an obscene tennis match.

"You, too," I tell her. "Get the fuck out of my house. You think he's not going to cheat on you, sweetheart? I got news for you. Cheaters cheat."

She shrinks back, covering herself in embarrassment and reaches for a towel.

I throw out a hand over them and say, "Oh, no. You can drip your shame right out the front door for all I care. Don't you dare touch my towels. Get. Out."

Am I being cruel? Maybe. But I have no fucks left to give.

As she runs from the bathroom, I step down and turn the water off with enough force I'm surprised the knob doesn't break off in my hand. I stand there, fuming, until I hear the door slam and the screech of tires as they speed away in Ben's sports car.

I should have known he wanted to impress other women when he talked me into that expensive thing, while I continued to drive my old, faithful, beat-up sedan. He always had a way of making me side with him. Even when I should have known better.

I walk to the hall bath. There is no way in hell I'm using the one they just violated. Yanking off the robe that was a gift from Ben, I stuff it into the small trash can and crank the water as hot as I can stand it. I step in and sink to the floor of the tub, the raw, boiling anger giving way to devastation.

I wrap my arms around my knees in a futile attempt to contain my hemorrhaging heart, and rock myself beneath the spray. I thought I would be coming home to safety, to reassurance. That Ben would help me figure out my next steps.

Hope swirls down the drain.

Without him, I don't know how I'm going to continue my research, or even finish my degree, with both of us in the same damn department. If the world of botany is small, ethnobotany is a microcosm within it.

Sure, I have a picture that might be enough to get him in trouble. But in the male-dominated world of academia, all it would probably earn him is a slap on the wrist with a sly wink and a quiet warning to be more discreet next time.

But even worse, I still haven't found the plant. The doctorate was part of it, yes, but the real reason was something far more personal. Ben knew I believed that the enzymes in the *Silene vitalis* held potential for treating the disease that killed my mother. What he didn't know, what I had never told him, was that I have the same gene. I could barely even admit it to myself.

I sit in the shower until the water runs cold, chasing me out, and go in search of a drink. I'll allow myself one night for an epic pity party where I can ugly cry until I'm empty, and then tomorrow I'll figure out a path forward. Alone. I can do this—I *must* do this— with or without him.

I reach for my favorite robe, but when I see it stuffed in the trash, the tears return with a vengeance. Breaking my own rule, I use the fancy decorative guest towels and then trudge to my room to find the most comfortable sweats I own.

When I open my drawer, I freeze, finding the pictures Ben must have hidden away there. I pull out all the frames that had once lined our dresser—snapshots of us frozen in time. I flip through them one by one, and a pattern emerges that I hadn't noticed before tonight.

Every photo highlights him. His achievements. His awards. His work. Always him. In each one, I'm there, yes, but I'm not looking at the camera. I'm looking at him, adoringly. As if I existed only in relation to his light, a supporting player in my own life.

I had continually helped him move forward, prioritized his success over mine. His research and doctorate. Then, his appointment as a professor. Hell, even our engagement and wedding date had been scheduled to accommodate his academic calendar. Not my timeline. I would've married him years ago.

I flip to the last photo, our engagement party, and there she is.

The girl from the bathroom stands at the edge of the group that surrounds us. Everyone else is smiling, cheering. But not her. Her lips are pressed into a hard line, her hands clenched into fists at her side. I never would've noticed it before. But now that I've seen it, it's so damn obvious. She's been there all along in the sidewings.

I thought Ben and I were equally devoted not just to each other, but also to our work and shared future. But now I see the truth: it was painfully one-sided.

I pull on my favorite sweats, then gather the pictures to my chest, and storm outside to the backyard. The fire pit is still loaded with the wood we never had the chance to use. With a grim little smile, I dump them on top and head into the garage, grab a lighter, and the gas can from the mower.

Returning like a woman on a mission, I pour a heavy dose of accelerant onto the sad pile. I pick up one picture and light the edge. Orange flames lick their way up the cardboard and I toss it in. A satisfying whoosh rises from the pit, a plume of heat and fury, and I let out a victorious whoop.

"Yeah! Take that, fucker!" I shout into the night.

Now that I've had a taste, I want more.

Marching through the house, I dump out a laundry basket onto the floor and start filling it with Ben's things. His favorite hat. His entire underwear drawer. The photo albums I had lovingly made of our years together. His precious collection of journals he'd been published in.

Passing through the kitchen, I toss a bag of chips on top, a tub of ice cream with a spoon, and the bottle of expensive tequila he'd been saving for a "special occasion." After all, I think this qualifies.

Back outside, I flop into one of the Adirondack chairs Ben insisted we buy last summer because they looked good. I try to get comfortable in it, but I've always hated them. I wrestle my way out, turn around, and hurl the damn thing across the lawn. It doesn't go far, but the crack of wood splitting as it lands is deeply satisfying.

I fetch a folding chair from the garage, wrap myself in a blanket, and settle in beside the fire. As the flames start to die back down, I feed them piece by piece—his journals, his underwear, and the photo albums. As the pieces of my life burn to ash, I work my way through the ice cream, the chips, and the booze, drinking straight from the bottle.

"Cheers, fucker," I mutter, raising it in a mock toast.

Despite my best efforts, nothing fills the aching hollowness his betrayal has left inside me. The throbbing emptiness spills over, carving hot, salty tracks down my cheeks. I toss his final pair of underwear into the fire, surprised to find the basket as empty as the bottle of tequila.

Pulling the blanket tighter around my shoulders, I let my fuzzy gaze drift to the edge of the woods. Even though I'm half a world away, I find myself scanning for those silver eyes again. Their absence triggers an ache within me—irrational, impossible, and yet so visceral.

A desperate, relentless need to see them again curls in my

gut, even in this drunken, grief-slicked haze. There is nothing left for me here. The life I built is gone. And if I don't find that plant, things will only get worse.

The solution floats to me like a whisper on the crackle of the fire. With a slurred giggle and a hiccup, I pick up my phone and finally start making decisions for me.

CHAPTER THREE

With a loud groan, I grip my head and squinch my eyes shut. My body protests spending the night on the hard ground, and my mouth feels like I ate a bag of cotton balls. The thought of eating anything makes my stomach lurch.

I crack open my eyes and survey the damage around me—a broken Adirondack chair, a melted tub of ice cream, and a very empty bottle of tequila. Scrubbing my hands over my face, I smooth them back through my hair to wind it into a knot and find the missing ice cream spoon stuck in my curls. I pick up the empty container to throw it away.

Heading inside, a whiff of last night's mint chocolate chip hits my nose. My stomach heaves in protest, and I pause to empty it into the bushes. With that cheerful start to my morning, I head back to my room, gather my toiletries, and go to the guest bath.

I still can't face my bathroom with the image of Ben's betrayal so fresh. I brush my teeth, chasing the resurrection of the tequila away, then sink into the comfort of a long, hot shower.

Part of me wants to stay here in the sweet-smelling steam, hide away from the reality waiting just beyond the curtain, maybe let the warm water wash it down the drain.

But another part of me is ready to move on. Now that I've realized what I sacrificed for Ben and his success, I vow to make myself the priority. With one last deep breath, I shut off the water and step into my new life, starting with doing some laundry.

While I wait, I choke down some tea and toast, missing the sweet chai of India, then stand at the kitchen sink, staring out the window at the edge of the woods as the rain begins to fall, lost in thought.

The harsh buzz of the dryer pulls me back. I fold my clothes and carry them to the closet but can't bring myself to put them away. As much as I don't want to stay in this house—this mausoleum of my failed relationship—I don't know where else to go.

All of my friends were our friends, and as I run through the list of people I might call, I realize I don't have anyone. The friends I had from college drifted away while I focused all my attention on Ben.

And now, I can't help but wonder if that wasn't intentional on his part.

I'd been the only child of a single mother, gone too soon from the same hereditary disease I'm trying to escape. It had been so easy for Ben to become my whole world. Without him, I have nothing.

The thought stops me cold.

I consider looking for another bottle or burning something else, but instead I retreat to the guest bed and curl into the blankets. I silence my phone. No interruptions. Just the welcoming escape of sleep.

When I wake, the sun is setting. I grope for my phone and squint at the too-bright screen in the dim room. Notifications of dozens of missed calls and texts from Ben light up the screen.

I'm not ready to hear his voice, so I open the messages first.

They're exactly what I expected—apologies, excuses, more lies. I pocket the phone and head to the kitchen, popping a frozen pizza into the oven. While it cooks, I pull out my phone again to start the search for a new place to live.

That's when I notice another notification. Not from Ben, but the airline I flew home on, reminding me to check in for a flight tomorrow.

I frown, confused. What flight?

Opening the app, I stare at the screen in disbelief. In my rage-fueled, tequila-soaked haze last night, I'd bought a one-way ticket —right back to India. And it leaves in less than twenty-four hours.

On one hand, it's nonrefundable. And I tell myself, if I go back, I can keep looking for the elusive *Silene vitalis*. It's not the mysterious eyes drawing me in again—not at all. It's only the plant, the cure to ensure my survival.

On the other hand, I could stay here. Try to rebuild my life and salvage my academic career. Mourn the loss of my relationship.

"Good thing I didn't put everything away," I mutter, the decision already made.

I tap *Check In*, surprised, and a little impressed, to see that drunk-me had splurged on a first-class ticket.

Sitting down with my pizza, I make a list of what needs to be done to leave my life here behind. I'll keep only what I can't live without from the house and stash it all in a storage facility. After I make a call and secure a unit, I repack my travel gear, ditching the things I didn't use before. I'm amazed at how much more efficient my backpack feels this time around.

With my bags packed and tomorrow planned, I go to sleep in this house for the last time. My dreams, once again, are haunted by silver eyes.

Anticipation has me out of bed before my alarm goes off. I make French press coffee, probably the last I'll have for a while, then head to the garage.

I empty every tub and container pathologically organized by Ben into a messy pile on the floor, then make my way through the house to gather the things I want to keep. A few of my favorite kitchen gadgets, most of my clothes, several boxes of books, and a few sentimental items.

Packing the car to the brim only requires one trip to the storage shed. Despite renting the smallest one, my belongings take up less than half.

Pride at my minimalism wars with the disappointment that this is all I have to show for my thirty-odd years. If I'd met my academic goals, maybe it wouldn't sting so much. But what do I have?

I run through a mental checklist. A few tubs of stuff. A failed relationship. No family. No friends. No doctorate. An unsuccessful research expedition. A bruised ego. A broken heart.

It's depressing.

But then, a memory of my mom surfaces, her voice soft but certain. *Sometimes the only place left to go is up, honey.*

I realize I have nothing left to lose. And with that comes the sweetest feeling I've known in years—freedom. I can go anywhere. Do anything. And that realization bolsters my mood.

Securing the lock on the storage unit, I head back to the house for one last sweep before I say goodbye to this life to chase the *Silene vitalis* and my chance at survival.

My mood is short lived. Disgust pools in my gut as I round the bend and see Ben's car in the driveway. Guarded, I walk inside to find him on the couch, elbows on knees, head in his hands.

"Dahlia, please," he whines, looking up at me as I come in. "I didn't mean to hurt you."

I stare at him. Flat. Numb. Shocked only by the fact that I feel nothing at all.

He stands and crosses the room, arms outstretched. As he reaches for my hands, I step back and snarl, "Don't touch me."

"It was one night. I was weak and lonely without you. We've never been apart for that long. Please, Dahlia, please forgive me," he says.

It sounds sincere. His voice even has that little quaver. But I've known this man for too many years. I know his tells.

He spins the ring on his right hand and raises his left eyebrow. He only does that when he's annoyed.

I've seen him use it on the dean, on the donors he calls "stupid rich people," on students without low cut shirts and perky smiles who dare ask questions. And now he's using it on me.

I play along.

"Why, Ben?" I ask quietly. "Why should I forgive you?"

I edge back toward the door. Nothing in this house is worth a confrontation, and the hair on the back of my neck is standing on end. I see the flicker of rage behind his eyes before he smooths his face back into that practiced mask.

"Dahlia, we've been together for years. We've both invested

in this relationship. Please, don't throw away everything we've built over one stupid mistake. It meant nothing. You mean everything. I've sacrificed so much for you. For us."

I back up another step, the carpet giving way to the linoleum of the foyer under my feet. He makes it sound like we're business partners. Like I'm an investment. Like love was nothing more than a footnote.

"Ben," I say, voice pleading, only trying to buy more time, as I shift my weight, inching toward the door.

His eyes narrow and his jaw clenches.

I've rarely seen him angry—he's too intelligent to be ruled by emotion. But something's shifted. Something's wrong. Because this doesn't feel like heartbreak. It feels like control slipping away.

"Dolly," he says, voice softening as he uses the nickname I've always hated, "we're so close. So close to realizing our dreams. Let's go back together. I can help you find the plant."

"The plant?" I echo. That's what this is about?

He hadn't wanted to go with me. Laughed at my theories. Scoffed at "roughing it" in the mountains. And now he believes? Now he wants to help?

No, something's off. As I stand there trying to piece it together, he lunges and grabs my wrist in a bruising grip.

But I've been hiking in high altitudes for months. I'm stronger than I was. Quicker. And, I'm mad. Just who the hell does he think he is?

My free hand finds the handle and, with a jerk, I throw the door open right into his face. A satisfying thunk is followed by a shrill shriek.

"My nose! You broke my fucking nose!" he squeals, clutching his face, blood streaming through his fingers.

I don't stick around to enjoy the win, but run to my car, fling myself inside, and slam the locks down. Backing out of the driveway, I grind the gears and clip the curb as I take off. One hand on the wheel, the other orders a ride to pick me up at the storage lot where I'll leave my car.

Only when Ben doesn't appear in the rearview mirror do I ease up on the gas, thankful to be putting a continent between us. In a million years, I never would've imagined this ending to our story. How could I not have seen this coming? I never dreamed Ben would cheat on me, much less physically attack me. Tears blur my vision, but I blink them away and focus on the road ahead.

When I pull into the lot, I grab my purse and wait, heart hammering. Every set of headlights tightens my chest until one pulls up with the familiar glow of an Uber sign. I exhale and grab my things.

I can't help but scan the surrounding area one last time as the driver loads my luggage in the trunk. When he slams the lid, I jump. He shoots me a worried glance, but I give him a weak smile and climb in. And just like that, I'm on my way to the airport, back to the mountains, and far, far away from this dumpster fire.

CHAPTER FOUR

Despite being exhausted, I can't sleep on the first leg of my journey. Every sound jerks me upright, adrenaline still coursing through my veins. The caffeine from the two lattes I definitely shouldn't have had back at the airport leave me feeling shaky and slightly nauseous.

I flip through books on my phone, but I can't focus. Even an audiobook can't hold my attention as my ears keep listening for danger. Despite the miles that rack up behind me, I can't shake the feeling I haven't seen the last of Ben.

We were together long enough that I know how tenacious he is. I go back through the years in my mind, trying to pinpoint where it all went wrong. Did he ever love me? Or was I always just a pawn?

I curse myself for being so naive, so trusting. He was my whole world. Everything had been for him. Now that I'm out from under his thumb, a new picture comes into focus. One where I finally see who Ben really is. The changes were so slow, so subtle, I hadn't even realized what was happening. I was the proverbial frog in boiling water.

Never again will I be subservient, or put someone else's needs ahead of my own. He taught me that I'm alone in this world, and if anyone's going to take care of me, it has to be me. Nothing like flying to the other side of the world to make that a priority.

By the time I get off the second plane, find my luggage, and meet the jeep I hired online during a layover, there's a new confidence in my step. I can only hope the ten-hour drive back to the mountain village goes quickly.

The first few hours are filled with bouncing roads and switchbacks. I try to upload my notes and maps to my computer, but the terrain is too rough. Instead, I pull out the originals, flipping through the weathered pages in my lap.

When we stop for lunch and a bathroom break at a roadside food stand, I unfold from the jeep with a groan, rubbing my sore back. A steaming cup of chai warms my hands, and for a moment, I'm transported back in time—holding a tiny clay mug as moonlight bathed the trees and those mysterious silver eyes flashed at me in the darkness.

I'm torn between hoping I'll see them again and praying my return will be distraction-free. With winter closing in and my resources stretched, I don't know how long I have this time.

At least I'd been smart enough not to give Ben access to the small inheritance my mother left me. Thinking of her brings a tightness to my throat. I've missed her for years, but I've never felt as alone as I do now.

The approaching winter isn't the only ticking clock I'm racing against. The need for this plant is more than academic. I can't let myself imagine what will happen if I fail again—or worse, if I'm wrong about its properties.

We load back into the jeep, and I force my thoughts elsewhere. I manifest hiking through unforgiving terrain, scanning for silvery green leaves and iridescent petals. A flash of color catches the sun. I run to it, fall to my knees, and cup the blossom in my hands. Its luminescent blue-violet matches my own unusual eye color, another gift from my mother.

Just as I begin to harvest it, my head jerks up to find we've arrived. I must have drifted off, lulled by exhaustion. I can't believe it, but in just a few days, I'm back at the very same guest house in the mountain town of Migdhari.

I walk inside, the scent of incense curling through the air. The owner looks up, mouth open in shock, then breaks into a warm, crinkled smile.

"Dahlia-ji! I thought you had returned home." Tenzig hurries over and presses his hands together with a slight bow. "Namaste."

"Namaste," I reply. With a sad smile, I add, "I did."

"The mountains have called you back," he says with a knowing look. "So, you must answer. You are tired. Come, I will show you to your room."

I follow him gratefully, his kindness like a balm to my bruised and battered heart. I'm thrilled when he opens the door to the same room I'd stayed in before. The familiar walls feel more like home than the house I just fled.

"Come to the lounge when you are ready for tea," he says gently as he leaves.

I unpack and sit on the bed, staring out at the water and woods beyond. Last time, I had searched only this side of the river. But something in those far-off trees calls to me, pulling at some deep, wordless place.

Tomorrow, I'll ask Sita to guide me again, this time across the water. Although all I want to do is fall into this bed, I could really use a friendly face. So I bundle up and head back to the lounge for tea, hoping it will thaw the frozen hollow where my heart should be.

No matter how tightly I pull my coat, the wind sneaks icy tendrils under my hood and along the hem of my parka. The temperature seems colder than even when I left, leaving no doubt that winter is coming.

Inside once more, I stretch my hands toward the fire's comforting glow. Tenzig sits beside me, passing me a steaming cup of chai.

After a long silence, I ask, "Tenzig, do you know if Sita is available to guide me again?"

"I believe so. She will be back in the morning, and you can ask her then." His gaze softens. "You have come back for the plant?"

I nod, staring off into the fire. The memory of those eyes, glittering and watchful, presses against my skin again. Now that I'm back, I can feel them stronger than ever.

I should feel uneasy. Instead, I feel a slow-burning anticipation. The kind of shiver that caresses like a lover's touch. A flicker of heat low in my belly. That gaze promised something wild. Something consuming.

The desire pooling within me is unexpected, but undeniable. I haven't just been craving sex, but intimacy. A true connection. Space to explore my body, my wants, my limits. With Ben, things had been... fine. Slotted into rare moments between deadlines. But every time I tried to deepen it, he dismissed me.

So, eventually, I stopped trying.

And even when we did have sex, something was missing. Like we were both just going through the motions.

Now, I know why.

I deserve someone who'll help me not only explore my sexuality, give me a safe space to experiment and uncover everything my body has to offer, but offer a genuine connection, a meeting of the heart and soul.

Not that I expect to find that here, high in the Himalayas.

Tenzig gently calls my name again, pulling me out of my thoughts and back to the present.

"Sorry, it's been such a long day," I murmur, hoping my longing doesn't show on my face.

He only smiles and bids me goodnight.

I walk back to my room and barely make it under the quilt before I fall asleep.

CHAPTER FIVE

I had every intention of waking early to find Sita. But my body, finally feeling safe, had other plans. When I stretch and roll over, the golden light of sunset pours through the window.

I hurry to the lounge to look for her, but Tenzig directs me to the fire pit outside. A new group of visitors huddles there, likely the last before the snow makes travel impossible. Sita moves among them, passing out steaming cups of chai.

Kicking myself for wasting a whole day, I hover near the fire until she's finished with her hostess duties. When she finally joins me, her warm smile reassures me.

I still apologize, "Sita, I'm so sorry I slept the day away!"

She laughs softly. "Please, do not apologize. I didn't think to ever see you again, *didi*."

The nickname for sister draws a smile. She truly feels like one. Not just a guide in my search, but a steady force through every lead and subsequent letdown. She's helped me navigate both the terrain and my own disappointments.

"Honestly, I didn't expect to ever be back, much less so soon. But here I am. We *must* find the plant, Sita."

She looks at me with quiet sympathy. She knows what's at stake.

"I feel like we need to search there," I say, pointing. "Across the river."

Her expression darkens. She gently lowers my hand, then draws a protective symbol in the air.

"Dahlia, I know how badly you need this plant. But we must not cross the sacred Migaia."

"Why not?" I frown. "We've searched everywhere else."

She shakes her head, eyes wide. "Please, don't ask me again tonight."

Her fear is out of character. We'd trekked cliffs and waterfalls together, agile as mountain goats. She's always been fearless. But now, just looking across the river, she seems shaken.

I don't press. Not yet.

We sit in silence, watching the fire burn down as darkness settles around us, the days already growing shorter. The other tourists drift off to bed until just one young man remains.

Sita excuses herself to place hot water bottles in my bed, fussing over me catching a chill. I smile at her retreating form, grateful beyond words to be with her again. It feels good to have someone care about me.

The man flashes me a grin as we're left alone. I smile back, which has him coming to sit beside me. His British accent is charming as he makes small talk, but I can't concentrate.

I feel something behind me, but this time, it isn't sensual. It's watchful and possessive. Territorial even.

I glance over my shoulder to find nothing but darkness. When I turn back, the man cocks his head at me as I mumble, "Thought I heard something."

He leans around me to peer into the night, balancing with a hand on my knee, saying, "I didn't hear anything."

I freeze, not because I feel threatened, but because I've forgotten how to read moments like this. Is he flirting? Or just being friendly?

Before I can decide, a thunderous crash exploding from the trees behind us has both of us leaping to our feet and spinning around. I scan the forest, searching for movement, but see nothing.

"Well, I definitely heard that," he says with a nervous chuckle. "I think that's our cue for bed."

"Yes," I murmur, still staring into the dark. "I think you're right."

Sita returns, eyes flicking between us. "Everything okay?"

"Yes, goodnight," the man says uneasily and heads off.

"Sita, there was a huge crash over there," I explain, pointing off in the direction the sound had come from.

She grabs my hand without a word and drags me back to my room. Once inside, she closes the door and leans against it.

"Sita?" I ask softly. "Are you okay?"

She gestures to the bed. We sit, and her eyes flick to the window that overlooks the forest.

"Didi," she says quietly. "There's a reason we haven't searched those woods. What you heard—it's not unusual here."

My heart stutters. "What do you mean?"

She hesitates before saying, "The mountains have their own

secrets, Dahlia. We call it the Migoi. Some say it's a myth. But I know better."

"You mean… Yetis?" I half-laugh, as I recall the local legends.

Her expression hardens. "The Migoi isn't the Western creature you imagine. It's a spirit. A guardian. Sometimes it helps. Sometimes it warns. And sometimes…"

Her voice trails off.

I lean forward. "You believe they're real?"

She nods. "I know they are. Most people leave when winter comes, but my family has always stayed here. We've seen tracks and other signs of a large creature. Too big to be a man. When we have enough, or when we have no choice but to enter those woods, we leave offerings."

She's quiet, staring out the window but her eyes are unfocused. After a few beats she continues. "One winter was so harsh, we nearly ran out of fuel and thought we'd freeze to death. But the next morning, we found wood stacked outside. So much wood, Dahlia. No man could've done that overnight."

She blinks away the memories and meets my eyes. "I listen to the mountains, to the earth. And I respect the Migoi."

I whisper, "So what we heard tonight… was that a warning?"

"Maybe. Or maybe it was just passing through." Her eyes dart back to the window. "But even without the Migoi, the forest across the river is dangerous—wild animals, avalanches, even harsher terrain than what we've already explored."

I swallow hard, realizing the weight of her words and say softly, "Sita, it's the only place we haven't searched. I *have* to go."

She sighs. "We will go back to the ashram first and ask again. Then, we'll see. Now, sleep."

She squeezes my hand. "We'll leave at first light."

CHAPTER SIX

The cold wind turns freezing as we finish our hike to the ashram. Despite my previous expedition conditioning me to the harsh terrain, today's pace leaves me panting in the thin air as we try to outrun the snow-laced sky.

Once we arrive, we are met with disappointment more bitter than the weather. After much cajoling and heartfelt pleas from Sita, one of the yogis admits he has heard a story of the plant I am looking for, but it is in a holy place he cannot, or will not, reveal.

No matter. I know it's across the river in the forbidden woods. Just as I know, despite the legends of the Migoi and the other dangers Sita warned me about, I must go there.

"Let's head back so I can update my notes," I tell Sita. I'm not lying, but the real reason to return is my plan to sneak into the forest at first light. Alone.

I'm not scared of the terrain, the weather, or even the Migoi, who is probably nothing more than the stories of Bigfoot back home—a tuft of fur, a misread footprint, a legend born of shadows.

Sita had never actually seen one, and as for the firewood? It must have been some neighbors who helped her family.

If I sneak out early every morning, I'll have a few hours to explore and get back before it gets too dark or cold. It's a desperate plan, but it's the only one I have.

Sita begs me to spend the night at the ashram with the threatening weather, but I'm desperate to start my search tomorrow. If we stay here tonight, it'll be another day wasted.

"It's all downhill from here," I remind her. "We have plenty of time to get back. Please, Sita."

At last she agrees, and we thank our hosts and depart for home. After the warmth of the ashram, the mountain air seems even colder. The normally expansive sky is a threatening gray that sends us scurrying down the trail.

Just as we lose sight of the building, fat, fluffy flakes begin falling. White blankets the ground, crunching under our boots as we pick up our pace.

"Dahlia, we're halfway between the ashram and home. I think we should keep going, since downhill will be easier," Sita says as the snow coalesces around us.

"I'm so sorry I pushed us to go," I say.

"No need to apologize. I agreed. Let's just focus on getting home as quickly and safely as possible."

She squeezes my arm with a smile, but I see the worry in her eyes. She's lived in these mountains all of her life, and I can tell she's trying not to scare me.

Eyes locked on the trail ahead, I push forward as fast as I dare, carefully planting each step. The once whimsical snowflakes now swirl with a menacing urgency.

As the temperature continues to plummet, I keep my eyes laser focused on Sita's vibrant jacket—my only beacon in the sea of white. The wind bites at any exposed skin and my fingers and toes throb with encroaching numbness. Each step becomes a battle. I stumble, my foot skidding off a hidden rock, and let out a startled yelp.

The second it takes to regain my balance is all it takes for Sita to vanish into the storm.

"Sita?" I call.

No answer.

I hurry forward a few steps, thinking she'll reappear, but she doesn't. I spin in a circle, blinking against the white out.

"Sita!" I yell, again and again.

Shivering, I remember my mother's childhood advice. *If you get lost, stay where you are. Someone will find you.*

I stand still, calling out every few seconds. But within minutes, my voice is hoarse, and I can no longer force it through my chattering teeth. I have to move or I'll freeze.

I test my footing to see which way slopes downward and start in that direction with slow, cautious steps. Disoriented, I try to map the trail in my head, but I'm well and truly lost. I can't see a thing.

Too late, I realize my next step lands on nothing but thin air.

On instinct, I cover my face and head, curling tight as I tumble. Snow and debris churn around me as I freefall until a violent thud knocks the breath from my lungs. Time stretches as I lay stunned, until I finally cough, dragging in air.

I try to move my arms and legs, but it's impossible. I'm trapped. Buried alive.

Focusing on just one limb, I start wiggling my right arm where it's still curled protectively around my face. Slowly, I create a tiny pocket.

Panic rises, but I fight it back. *Think, Dahlia. Think.*

The urge to yell for Sita wars with the need to conserve oxygen. I slow my breathing, trying to protect what little air I have. All too soon my limbs grow heavier and a tingling creeps up my legs. If I don't suffocate, I'll freeze to death. Using every ounce of willpower I possess, I slow my breathing even more.

I can't blindly fight my way out of this. I need to figure out which direction I am facing. I work up what little saliva is in my mouth and spit. It falls straight down.

Digging upward isn't an option, so I'll need to somehow back myself out. The thought brings wildly inappropriate lyrics to mind as a bizarre soundtrack to the grim situation. I start nodding my head to the beat and try to wriggle my body, booty end first, muttering, "Back that ass up."

Between the freezing cold sapping my energy and the weight of the snow dragging me towards exhaustion, I debate giving up. Maybe freezing to death won't be that bad.

But the song plays on in my mind, and somehow it gives me the strength to dig deeper, tap into some hidden well of strength, and just keep shaking that ass. Every gyration confirming I'm not ready to die yet. Every thrust of my hips declaring I haven't come all this way to give up now.

Suddenly, something shifts, and an icy blast hits my bottom, sneaking tendrils up the back of my parka.

"No, shit, nineties rap for the win," I chatter out.

Delicious icy air flows past my body and floods my lungs, but no matter how much I tell my body that I need just a few more seconds of energy, it will not listen. The wind whispers to just rest, and I nod. That twerking was a lot of work, I think as my eyes drift closed.

"Something, something, back that ass up," I mumble, slower now, even my lips too cold and tired to move.

And then someone grabs said ass and pulls. Sita must have found me. That was way too close. I flop onto my back, staring at the sky. Snowflakes land on my face, but I barely feel them.

"Thank you," I whisper, almost too exhausted to speak.

A dark shape looms over me, but the eyes that meet mine aren't Sita's. Instead I find the familiar swirling silver that has plagued my dreams.

And they belong to a Migoi.

"Fuck," I breathe.

This is bad. Really, really bad. I wonder if staying buried alive would have been safer. And yet, I could swear amusement flickers in its gaze at my curse.

Its deep set eyes are large and luminescent, laced with the frost and misty grey. They are full of secrets and heavy with the weight of time. I close my own, willing the shock-induced hallucination away, but when I reopen them—it's still there, staring down at me.

"Uh, hi. Thanks. Thank you for saving me," I whisper. "I didn't mean to enter your territory. I mean you no harm."

The Migoi blinks slowly. I can't stop staring at the immense shaggy head, the wild white fur, and those mesmerizing eyes.

I should be terrified, but I'm mostly just... cold. Another shiver overtakes me, my teeth chattering so loudly I can't control it.

The Migoi's gaze sharpens. It tilts its head, then with a huff, scoops me up against its massive body.

A yelp escapes me but I collect myself and stammer out, "Thank you."

It comes out as more of a question than a statement. I think I hear a grunt in reply as it pulls me closer, so much heat radiating off its body that it permeates through my clothes. My fingers and toes tingle painfully at the return of circulation, but I let out a soft moan at the lifesaving warmth that cushions me against the howling storm around us.

After a particularly brutal gust of wind, the creature pulls me even closer, and its fur somehow seems to grow longer, wrapping around me like the softest blanket. Between its body heat and my unexpected cocoon, I give in to the post near death exhaustion and sleep.

CHAPTER SEVEN

I drift in and out of consciousness, sometimes awakened by the howl of wind, sometimes by the pins and needles of returning circulation. But each time, I'm rocked back to sleep by the steady, rhythmic stride of my walking, heated fur blanket.

I can only hope we're headed back to Migdhari, and that Sita somehow made it home.

But we're going up when I think we should be heading back

down. I can feel it in the change of the air, the way the creature's muscles flex against me and my weight shifts as we climb. My mother's voice echoes in my memory, soft and certain. *Sometimes the only way left to go is up, honey.*

Disoriented, I bury my face deeper into the Migoi's soft fur, craving the warmth after my icy brush with death. A low growl vibrates against my cheek. I freeze, worried I've upset him, but then an enormous hand cups the back of my head, as if encouraging me to repeat the motion.

I nuzzle the creature again, and the deep, appreciative sound that follows is unmistakably male.

Curious, I slip off my gloves and sink my fingers into the dense fur, finding the source of the heat—his skin, smooth like velvet under the dense fur. A moan escapes me at the decadent heat, and his arms flex, pulling me tighter.

And suddenly, I'm burning.

It's wrong—this is a mythical creature, not a man—but my body doesn't seem to care. I blame the adrenaline, the trauma, the comfort of warm, strong arms after nearly dying for the hunger pooling between my thighs.

I squeeze my legs together, ashamed, but the pressure only stokes the need. My cheeks flush. The heat, the safety, the primal power of the being holding me—it's overwhelming.

A deep rumble beneath my cheek freezes me. He knows. Oh, no, somehow he knows. I force myself to stay still, scarcely daring to breathe, but eventually, as nothing else happens, the steady cadence of his stride lulls me under once more.

A creeping chill wakes me some time later. I sit up slowly. The biting wind is gone, replaced by thick, mineral-rich air. Steam rises from a raised formation in ethereal wisps, curling toward a high ceiling where stalactites hang like frozen chandeliers in this hidden cathedral of stone and mist.

I stand with a groan and make my way over to the source of

the steam, a pool with bioluminescence dancing across its surface.

When I dip a finger in, heat and light shimmer in its wake. I swirl my hand through the warm water, surprised by the faint glowing trail it leaves behind.

Where am I?

A shape emerges from the shadows and coalesces into myth made flesh. Unsure what to do, I flutter my fingers in a little half-wave, then kick myself for making such a silly gesture at the legendary guardian of the mountains and forest.

The Migoi steps into the soft light, and I suck in an audible breath.

He is as ruggedly handsome as the harsh terrain he calls home. Still otherworldly, yes, but undeniably male. Tall, broad, carved from shadow and ice, every inch of him honed and hardened. High cheekbones, a straight nose, and a shock of white hair frames silver eyes that glow like moonlight over the snow-covered mountains.

He stands beside the rocky edge of the pool and dips a hand into the water, the steam curling around his skin. As he slicks his hair back with it, I find myself drifting forward. I don't realize my hand is outstretched until it makes contact with the hot, velvety plane of his abdomen, mere fuzz where before there was fur.

Running my fingers over the rippling muscles, I mutter, "The abdominal snowman."

Embarrassed by my boldness, I snatch my hand back and stare at the floor, but he gently lifts my chin.

He regards me with inscrutable intensity, and maybe a faint touch of amusement, brushing a calloused thumb over my bottom lip.

My breath catches at the feeling of his thickened skin on my lips and the mystery in his eyes. For being lost somewhere in the Himalayan mountains, I have never felt more found.

"Where are we?" I whisper.

His eyes drop to my lips and warm, reigniting the earlier desire that pooled in my belly. He's looking at me like I'm his next meal, and despite my brain screaming at me to run, I can't help but wonder what it would be like to be devoured by him.

The warm safety of the cave is a sharp contrast to my fall, the suffocating snow, and my close brush with death. I reach up and lay my hand against his arm. "You saved me."

He shoots me a very human smile as we stand with the steam curling up from the pool and filling the air between us. I'm not sure which is more surreal—this hidden oasis in the midst of the mountain's snowstorm, or this creature. But now I owe him my life.

I shiver, but not from the cold. Noticing, he gently tugs my hand and leads me up a path to the top of the pool. I follow, dazed, admiring the strength in his back, the curve of his spine, the frankly perfect ass that should not belong to a myth.

"That ass though," I mutter.

He stops abruptly, and I'm so focused on the view that I crash into him with a yelp and topple over.

CHAPTER EIGHT

W ater rushes over me, the weight of my wet clothes dragging me under. Panic bubbles up like the scream that escapes from my throat, but before I can even fight to surface on my own, he lifts me from the water like a rag doll, holding me against him as I sputter and gasp.

Marvelling at his reflexes, I cough, then mumble, "Sorry."

He raises an eyebrow. "How did you survive without me?"

My jaw drops. His voice is rough, as if dragged from the

heart of the mountain, hewn from the stones themselves, but his English is flawless.

Which means…

The singing. The abdominal snowman nickname. The ass comment.

He heard *everything*.

My cheeks flame as I mumble out the first response that comes to my mind. "To be fair, I don't usually almost die more than once a day."

"I rather enjoy you alive," he replies, setting me on my feet. The way his voice rumbles over the word *enjoy* reverberates deep in my core.

The water laps at my waist, and as I look down, I realize three things.

One—all I had to do to save myself was stand up in the shallow water. Instead, I panicked.

Two—for the first time in my life, I am very small. I barely reach his chest, and the water that pulled me under doesn't even make it past his thighs.

And that's how I end up staring directly at realization number three—giant mythical creatures have giant mythical cocks.

Oh. My. Gods.

And said cock is now close. Very close.

I can't help but stare. In awe. In curiosity. In want.

He begins to harden under my gaze, the already impressive member rising up through the air towards me as the long prominent veins on the shaft begin to pulse. Mortified, I snap my eyes away.

"Um, thanks again," I squeak, suddenly fascinated by the shimmering stalactites above us.

As he reaches out to unzip my coat, I bat his hand away and snap my eyes back to his. "Excuse me! Just because I had a little looky loo doesn't mean you can undress me."

He rolls his eyes and says, "Your clothes are soaked. You'll catch cold."

As if on cue, the clothes clinging wetly to my body above the warm waters start to cool, leeching the heat from my skin.

"Oh, of course. I'm sorry. You're right," I say sheepishly, and start peeling off layers, clumsy and shivering, aware of his eyes following my every movement. When I struggle to pull off my boot, he steps forward and uses a single claw to slice the tangled laces free. Feeling shy despite the dim light in the caverns, I strip but leave my soaked white tank and panties on.

I thrust my soggy pile at him and watch him vault out of the water with fluid ease. When he returns, his silver eyes fall to my peaked nipples blatantly visible through the thin wet fabric. His gaze turns molten, and my skin heats hotter than the water around us.

I let him take my hand and guide me deeper. The pool glows brighter here, and I trail my fingers through the glow, entranced, as a laugh escapes me—light and unguarded.

"Do that again," he says softly.

I look up, caught by the change in his voice. "Do what?"

"Laugh."

Then he sweeps me into his arms and spins me, pulling more laughter from my lips. For a moment, I forget everything. The snow and suffocation, betrayal and degrees, the elusive flower, even Ben, all just fall away.

Here I am warm and safe. Seen.

When I reach for his jaw, my fingers trembling, he goes still.

Our eyes meet.

And I realize with a start, I want him to kiss me. *Need* him to. I'm drowning again—but this time in pools of liquid silver heat, and the only thing that will save me is his kiss. I need him to breathe his air into me, to ease the tightness of suffocation gripping my chest for the third time today.

The already humid air thickens with the tension that blooms between us like a rare flower. Beautiful and exotic.

But instead of kissing me, his tongue traces his lower lip, a glint of pointed canines showing as he guides me deeper into the pool. The water begins to move, glowing and swirling as if alive. But I can't tear my eyes away from his.

In the deeper waters, a current flows over my body like a lover's hands. He positions me against a jet-like pulsing. It strokes my back, lower, until it pulses between my thighs, and my gasp is immediate.

He growls, low and feral, and spins me so my back is pressed to his chest. His rapidly-hardening cock rubs against the swell of my ass, thick and impossibly hot.

His hand slips beneath my tank to palm my breast. The other moves between my thighs, tugging my panties aside. The water finds me there, steaming and relentless, and I cry out as it pulses against me.

His voice is dark silk at the shell of my ear. "What was that song you were singing earlier?"

Song? What song? I can't answer him when all I can think about is his hands roving over my breasts. All I can feel is the heat of his impressive erection grinding against me. And that damn relentless water is driving me mad.

"Back that ass up?" he murmurs, every syllable drenched in wicked satisfaction.

Caught off guard, I laugh, but then he adjusts himself so that his monster cock is between my thighs. When he thrusts, my laugh trails off into a moan. Desperate for more, I cross my ankles and squeeze my knees, trapping him there, grinding down on him.

He groans, the sound vibrating through my back.

"That's it," he growls. "Let me feel how much your body weeps for me."

I reach down, attempting to fit my fingers around the thick, tapered head of his cock that protrudes past my legs. He pulses against my palm, and I stroke slowly, worshipfully, exploring every vein, every ridge that I can reach. Precum coats my fingertips like liquid fire.

His hand returns to my clit, working in perfect counterpoint to the jet. My hips shift, chasing the rhythm, hungry for more. They can't decide whether to try to grind down onto the girth between my thighs or seek out the pulsating water.

"Please," I whisper, the need raw in my voice.

He releases my sex and yanks my tank top to expose my breasts to his questing hands. He massages them, easily supporting my weight in the water so I can grind against him. I feel every ridge, every contour and pulsing ropelike vein along the iron shaft trapped between my thighs. My soaked tanktop clings to my curves, nipples taut against his palms. I am lust incarnate.

Ben always made me feel like I was too much. Too soft. Too needy. But this creature—he holds me like I'm perfect. Like I was made to be worshipped.

I moan, pussy dripping, thighs trembling. Sliding back and forth along his shaft until the tapered head nudging against my clit has me so close, but I can't get enough friction with the slick water.

His fingers twist into my hair, tilting my head back until I meet his gaze to find those silver storms swirling with hunger. His other hand slices my panties free with a quick flick of his claws, then slips inside me.

The first finger slides deep, thick and bold. I let out a deep groan at the feeling, my arousal even slicker than the water surrounding us. When he adds another, the stretch pulls a broken sound from my throat. But it's when he curls them inside me and his thumb returns to my clit that I shatter.

The climax rips through me like that damned avalanche. I clench around his fingers, limbs trembling, a cascade of cries and curses falling from my lips as he coaxes every aftershock from my shaking body.

He turns me to face him, a dark, satisfied smile showcasing his pointed canines. He lifts me easily, and my legs immediately wrap around his waist. His cock strains toward my entrance, swollen and impossibly thick. The fear he will split me in two pierces through my lust filled haze and must be clear on my face.

"You will take me," he says, voice like thunder. "But tonight, you take only my seed."

At last he claims my mouth in a kiss—hot, rough, consuming. His tongue plunges into my mouth, stroking mine, chasing every retreat, swallowing every sound I make. The sharp edge of his teeth just grazes my lips but has me moaning all over again.

His cock presses just barely inside, just the tip of the tapered head, and my lips part in a gasp at the exquisite stretch.

He groans into the kiss, one hand tangled in my hair, the other running down my back, over my ass, and moving lower until he's pressing a slick finger against my tightest opening. The water makes everything so damn slippery, and it slides in on a moan.

I feel desperate and wicked for all he is offering. All that I have wanted and desired, my secret fantasies safely hidden away for so long are being laid bare. I want him everywhere.

The fear of his size drifts away in the swirling water and the overwhelming sensations have me grinding down, chasing him, desperate for more.

He reaches down between us to pump his thick shaft while he uses his other hand to claim my ass with slow, advancing strokes.

Desire unfurls, dark and wild. I writhe against him, undone, desperately trying to get more of his monster cock inside of me, but even with my arousal and this mineral water, it just won't fit.

He breaks the kiss to pant against my cheek.

"You want me to claim every inch of your body," he growls, not a question but a declaration.

I nod, helpless, too consumed by the sensations to even speak, and it is his undoing.

His tip swells inside me, and then—release. Hot spurts pulse from his cock, shooting into me, branding me. It floods my channel, overflowing out of my entrance, hotter than even the water around us and my body responds, aching to draw it deeper. To be filled. Marked. Claimed, just as he said.

The deep pressure of the hot fluid has another climax crashing over me—stronger, wetter, wilder. I scream into the echoing cave, a raw sound of need and freedom and surrender.

But he's not done with me.

With a deep growl, he stalks over and balances me on the slick stone edge of the pool. My legs tremble as he lifts one over his shoulder.

"Keep my seed inside of you," he rasps, the possessiveness in his voice gathering like a snowstorm in my soul. "Hold it in your tight heat."

Before I can answer, he slides the head of his cock free. Thick, white cum drips from my entrance, and he tsks, swiping it up and using two thick fingers to push it back into me. He presses his other palm against the fullness of my belly like he's trying to imprint himself into my womb.

A feral moan tears from my throat. The sight of his release being stroked back into me, the way he watches me like I'm already his—it's too much.

My core flutters again, tightening. My thighs shake.

He doesn't stop.

One hand continues to stroke and fill me, while the other

slides up to caress my breast, teasing the nipple until it's hard and aching.

"I want you to feel me inside of you for days," he growls. "I want your body to crave me. Hunger for me. Weep for me."

My body jerks and locks around his fingers, a gush of liquid pleasure pulsing out to mix with his seed, the water, the heat. Weeping for him, just as he said.

He lowers his great shaggy head and sucks my breast into his mouth, laving my nipple with his tongue before switching to the other side. His fingers continue to pump into me, and the sound of my desire echoes off the water and into the cave around us.

It is so real and raw. I chase his fingers with my hips, my head falling back in ecstasy as I grip the ledge. I am pure need. He sinks his sharp teeth into my breast, and my screams echo in the cave, a primal cry of surrender as my pussy clenches tight, locking down on his large fingers. My limbs shake, and my vision blurs.

He holds me through it, strong arms anchoring me to him.

When I collapse against him, wrecked and boneless, he murmurs something soft in a language I don't know.

All I understand is I just had the best orgasm of my life.

With a Yeti.

And gods help me—I want more.

CHAPTER NINE

The Migoi carries me boneless and—I'm pretty sure—drooling out of the pool and into a smaller cavern where a fire burns merrily. My clothes and boots are laid neatly out to dry around it.

He sets me on my feet, swaying, and eases my tank top up and off from where it's bunched above my breasts. I push down the ruined scrap of red lace panties still clinging to my hips.

He steps back to stare, hunger carved into every line of his face and burning in his gaze. His silver eyes rake over every inch of me like he's starving.

My cheeks flush, heat prickling beneath my skin as I instinctively hunch forward, arms sliding in to cover the curves Ben always criticized.

The Migoi growls and swats my hands away.

"Mine."

The single word lands like a brand against my skin. Well, this might prove more complicated than I thought.

As much as I want to stay here and fuck the time away, I need to find the *Silene vitalis*. But I can't go anywhere. Not yet. Not while my only clothes are still dripping dry by the fire. Not while my muscles still shake from exertion. And certainly not while this primal creature looks at me like I hung the stars.

Maybe just a day or two more. Surely I deserve that after all that has happened.

When I sway again, he scoops me up with that now-familiar ease. His heat presses through me, his velvety skin soft against me. I could get used to this as a mode of transport, I think as he carries me to a massive bed heaped with furs and settles me down on the side facing the fire.

I reach for a pelt, but instead he pulls me closer against his chest. His rapidly-hardening length settles between the cleft of my thighs like it belongs there.

When I shiver, his velvety skin morphs into a thick pelt, and wraps around me like a blanket. Snug in my personal fur coat, with a living furnace at my back, I drift off to sleep.

I dream of silence, of suffocating, crushing white. The air in my lungs turns sharp and deadly. I know what's coming—my oxygen will run out while my strength fades. My mind whispers that this is how I die. Cold. Alone.

A scream claws its way up from my throat.

The bed rustles violently. I sit up just in time to see the Migoi crouched in front of me, claws extended, silver eyes reflecting the dim light of the fire as he scans the room for danger.

Every inch of him bristles. His fur is even longer, making him appear larger—like a startled cat built to kill. What would that be, a saber tooth tiger?

Despite the terror still pulsing in my veins, a surprised giggle slips from my mouth at the thought.

He whips his head around at the sound, and the look on his face strips the smile from mine. His expression is lethal. A pure apex predator.

This is the guardian the mountains fear.

Then he softens. The fur retracts, and his claws disappear. In the space of a breath, the beast fades, and the protector returns.

"I'm sorry," I whisper. "I was dreaming of the avalanche."

In an instant, he's beside me, pulling me into his arms and making me feel small, cherished.

"Tell me," he murmurs into my hair.

As he traces the tips of his claws up and down my spine, I say, "I was trapped. The dark... the silence. I couldn't move. Couldn't breathe. I knew I was going to die." My voice shakes. "I had to choose whether to give up or fight."

"But you *did* fight. That's how I found you. Singing something about backing your ass up. Poorly, I might add," he adds.

Despite myself, I laugh.

"If you hadn't saved me, I'd be dead," I say.

He turns my face to his. "No. You would never give up. You are a fighter."

"I don't know. I *was* giving up. And now..." I shrug helplessly. "I don't know what I have left to fight for. I have no one to go home to, and without my research, not only do I have no purpose, I have no chance."

He grips my chin, tilting my face up until his burning silver gaze pins me in place.

"You have *you* to fight for."

I look away, uncomfortable with his assertion. He believes in me more than I do. How sad is that?

"I just feel… lost," I say in a small voice.

"Then let me show you that you are still worth fighting for," he says. His voice brooks no argument.

"Okay," I whisper. I'm not sure what he means, but his tone says everything.

Still, he doesn't move.

"I need your trust. Completely," he says.

I study his face. This beautiful, fearsome creature that should have me terrified. But I'm not. He's seen me at my weakest, and he's still here. Piecing me back together.

"I trust you," I murmur. And I mean it.

He lowers his large forehead to mine, and we just sit in the moment. I realize this creature has shown me more kindness and compassion than Ben ever did. Tears prick at my eyes at the temporary nature of this relationship. I wish it could last forever.

He carries me again, this time into the tunnels. The firelight fades as we move deeper into the earth. The cave turns pitch black.

He sets me down in the absolute silence where the darkness pulses like a living, breathing thing.

My heartbeat fills the vacuum. I want to ask what we're doing, but a single finger brushes my lips. *Shhh.*

Then his disembodied voice echoes, as if the mountain itself is speaking. "I'm going to show you. Make you remember your worth."

The silence that follows is crushing. The darkness is suffocating. My skin prickles with phantom cold, and suddenly, I'm back beneath the snow.

My chest tightens. I try to regulate my ragged breathing, but my brain whispers *you're going to die, alone, in the dark.*

Just as panic threatens to consume me, I feel it.

Velvet fingertips. Brushing my skin. Light, slow, deliberate.

They trace my outline, pulling me into the present. I focus on the feeling—warm hands skating over my arms, my face, my curves. Drawing me back into my own body.

I'm not buried. I'm here.

His hand cups my face, then traces the shape of my lips. I remember how the sunlight reflects off my hair. My eyes twinkle with mischief. My face is so expressive that no, I can't hide my annoyance, but neither can I hide my joy, and that's a gift to share with the world.

Then his hand clamps down over my mouth and nose.

I freeze.

The other trails lower—down my breasts, over my belly, between my legs.

Panic spikes. I buck instinctively, heart racing. *Air.* I need air.

Then his fingers plunge inside me.

I cry out against his palm as two thick digits stretch me wide, curling inside with devastating precision to find some secret spot that has me blooming for him.

Fear and desire war in my blood, combining to form a new element, a hot and heady mixture.

And yet my traitorous body responds. The wet sounds of my arousal echo in the cavern. My hips grind wantonly against his hand. Pressure builds in my core, threatening to burst out of my body like the air that is trapped in my lungs.

Stars bloom in my vision.

Just as darkness threatens to take me, the orgasm hits— violent and overwhelming, splintering my fear into oblivion. I scream into his palm. I *fight*. I survive.

When I come back to my body from somewhere out in the stratosphere, I see the darkness of the cave isn't truly black at all —it's a thousand shifting shades of grey. I feel every contour of the stone floor against my skin. The air flows over my body, brushing against every fine hair, carrying with it the rich scent of the cave and the snow and pine scent of the Yeti's primal musk, mingled with my own heated arousal.

What I first mistook for sensory deprivation is, in fact, an overwhelming cascade of input. With a sudden burst of understanding, I wrench his hand away and gulp down a deep, sweet lungful of air. Sitting up, my chest heaving, I feel a grin stretch across my face, wild and unrestrained.

"I didn't just survive," I whisper, understanding coloring my voice with awe. "I came back. For this. For *me.*"

He's watching me. Silver eyes glowing. Proud. Hungry.

I launch myself at him.

He catches me and rolls to his back, pulling me atop him. My slick pussy glides up every ridge and dip of his stomach. He grabs my hips, positions me over his mouth, and *devours* me. I grind down into his face, hands tangled in his thick white hair as I hold on for dear life.

His growl vibrates through my core, reverberating into my belly. Wet heat, teeth, lips—he's merciless. I groan, as his mouth covers everything, lips, clit, ass, like he's claiming territory. His tongue spears inside me, and I ride his mouth shamelessly. His tongue is huge, bigger even than when he filled me with two of his fingers.

I lift and drop my hips, fucking his tongue, gasping as it snakes ever deeper, until the tip is caressing some undiscovered spot inside of me. My hardened clit brushes against his sharp teeth, and I break. It's loud. Messy. Raw.

He doesn't stop.

Even after I go still, he caresses my walls with his tongue until finally he slowly retreats to lick at me lazily, like he can't help himself. Like he needs every last drop.

"Please," I pant. "Let me touch you."

He lifts me gently, setting me on shaky feet.

"There is nothing I would love more," he murmurs. "But this was just for you."

With a smile, he pulls me gently by the hand. I try to keep up, but even with my sharpened senses, my smaller strides are no match for his sure and steady pace across the uneven cavern floor.

Noticing this, he scoops me into his arms once more, holding me close against his hot, velvety skin. I melt into him with a small, contented sigh. We pass the glowing pool and wind our way back through the tunnels until the firelight returns, flickering golden and familiar against the stone walls.

The warm embrace of arriving home surrounds me, and my cheeks ache with a smile that splits my face. But it quickly falls as I realize, this is only home for *now*. Not for long, just for now. A small slice of a temporary paradise.

He sets me down beside the hearth and hands me a cool jug of water. I drink greedily, only now realizing how thirsty I am. Then he offers a small basket filled with dried fruits, seeds, and nuts.

I eat slowly, watching him move around the cave. He tends to the fire, turns my boots near the flames, folds my now-dry clothes with surprising care.

Watching him in this oddly gentle and domestic scene has a dangerous ache blooming in my chest. The kind that says *stay*. Make this your forever home.

My body will be ready to leave soon. My clothes will be dry, and so will my boots. I can pick up the trail, head back to Migdhari, and keep chasing the *Silene vitalis*.

But the thought of leaving him feels… unbearable.

Despite the short amount of time we've shared, he sees me. All of me. More clearly than Ben ever did. More honestly than I've seen myself in years.

I lie down in the mountain of furs, full and warm and content in a way I didn't know I needed. The Migoi hums low under his breath as he tidies, something ancient and rhythmic in the sound. The softly crackling fire mixes with it to make the perfect, relaxing background soundtrack.

He returns to my side, lowering himself behind me where he curls his massive body around mine like a living shield. His heat seeps into my skin as his breath ghosts over the back of my neck.

I let myself sink into his arms, into this strange little world we've carved out of stone and ice. It feels so comfortable, so warm and safe. *Home* pulses again in my heart, more sensation than thought.

Gods help me—I don't want to go. Tomorrow, I'll start thinking again. Tomorrow, I'll figure out what I have to do. How to leave.

But tonight, I belong to him.

CHAPTER TEN

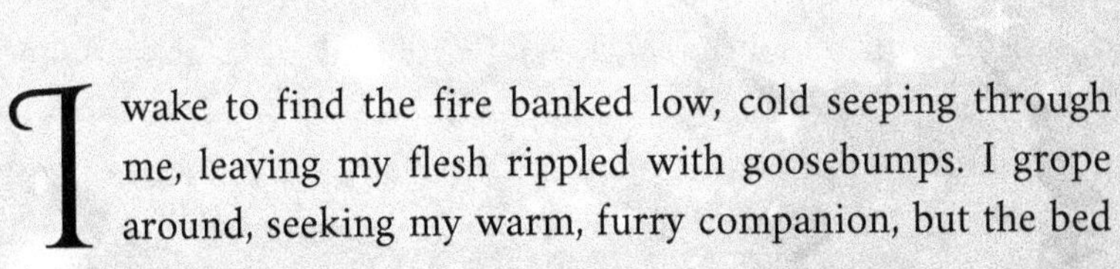

I wake to find the fire banked low, cold seeping through me, leaving my flesh rippled with goosebumps. I grope around, seeking my warm, furry companion, but the bed is empty.

I stand and stretch, crossing to where my clothes are neatly stacked. I slip them on, minus the ruined panties, and grab my boots. Sitting down, I cobble the laces back together from where he had cut them with his claw, a delicious shudder ghosting over me at the memory of what came next.

Looking for my missing Yeti, I venture out to the large pool, but not finding him, I spin in a slow circle and take in the expanse of the caves. I know better than to go wandering in the dark alone, risking getting hurt or lost. One end of the cave appears lighter though, so I head towards it.

As I walk and more light filters in, I see paintings lining the walls. Not quite as primitive as the famous cave paintings of France or Argentina but nor are they modern.

The pictures tell the story of the Migoi's world. The beginning starts with a Yeti and a woman with the moon. Perhaps a moon goddess is their creation story? It looks like at one time, there were more of his kind, and they do seem to be some sort of guardians or protectors of the forest, just like Sita had said.

As I follow the images and the light grows brighter, I come across one final image, a large Yeti, a slightly smaller one, and between them, a small furry object I can only assume is a baby. My heart tightens as I wonder what became not just of this family, but of all the Migoi on the walls.

A breeze pulls my attention, and I walk further towards the fresh air to find an exit. I slip out just in time for the sunset.

I stand for a moment, letting the beauty of this world wash over me. The never-ending sky is a welcome change after the confines of the caves. But not wanting the Migoi to worry at my absence, I turn to head back—only to find no trace of the entrance.

Confusion prickles through me. I haven't walked more than a few paces away, yet the opening is nowhere to be seen. Frowning, I step closer, but it's as if the cave has vanished entirely, leaving me standing alone in the wilderness.

Wrapping my arms around myself as the temperature plummets with the setting sun, I decide to stay put, not wanting to chance wandering away and getting lost. As I sit on the ground, the sounds of the forest start to surround me, and I feel... at peace. In fact, this is the happiest I've been since I can remember.

No frantic research, no Ben, no spiraling thoughts. Just the unique stillness that comes from being enveloped by nature rather than the noise of humanity. The calm quickly dissipates, and I sit up straighter, my senses sharpening as I strain to catch the subtle shift in the air around me.

Fear ghosts over my skin as I realize how defenseless I am, sitting out here alone in the darkening night. Maybe I should try to locate the cave again. I had been hoping the Migoi would come to find me, but now, I'm not so sure. At least physically, I felt a connection with him. And I thought there was something beyond even that, but perhaps he did this with all the women he rescued from avalanches?

Frowning, it dawns on me that I don't even know his name to call out for him. I stand up, determined to find the entrance when I hear a noise. Fear skitters down my spine as I freeze, hoping I can somehow escape whatever is out there.

The beautiful twilight has exchanged its dusty purple hue for a shadowy grey and black landscape as the light fades quickly. The forest noises which were soothing just a moment ago take on a sinister quality.

My heartbeat quickens as my primitive brain urges me to run. A low growl has me sprinting into action, racing towards where I think the cave's entrance must lie. I can't help but look back over my shoulder, wondering how much time I have to escape whatever is after me.

While my head is turned, I slam into a solid wall of heat and dense fur. The snow and pine scent of my Yeti surrounds me as a large arm sweeps me behind him to safety. He turns and lunges at the creature chasing me. I lean to the side, brave enough in his presence to see just what he is protecting me from.

A large wolf with raised hackles, gnashing teeth, and dripping saliva strains and snaps on his leash. I frown at such a ferocious thing being owned. Following the long leather lead, I trace it back to its owner, standing at the tree line, heavily cloaked and hooded.

The Migoi lets out a fierce roar, echoing through the forest. The wolf tucks its tail and runs behind its owner, clearly knowing it is not the alpha here. Despite the distance and the dim lighting, I see the man's face transform, sheer terror overtaking him as he falls to his knees.

At the low growling that continues to emanate from my savior, the man gets his feet under him, backing away while still bowed. He unties a sack at his waist and tosses it towards us, retreating to the safety of the woods.

The Yeti spins around to face me, confronting me with the sight of just how fearsome he is. He appears larger than I've ever seen him, muscles rippling with each heaving breath. His normally luminescent eyes are almost completely black in the darkness of the night, and his canines give him a wolfish appearance.

I should probably be stumbling backwards, away from this creature that is more beast than man in this moment. But I've had enough of doing what I should. Of shrinking myself down, listening to others, being practical, sensical. I want some damn *nonsense*. I want to be hedonistic and chase down my desires. It's time for me to be Dahlia fucking *Wilde*.

So instead of running away, I race forward and launch myself into the air, trusting his strong arms to catch me. And they do, a split second before our mouths crash into each other. I swallow his snarl with a moan as the sharp edge of his teeth drags over my lips and tongue, the tang of copper blooming on my tastebuds.

Burying my hands in his thick white hair, I angle my head to kiss him deeper. I'm so lost in the claim of his mouth that I barely notice the impact of the stone wall on my back as he slams me back against the mountain.

A grunt escapes me as he trails frenzied kisses down my neck, nipping at my pulse point. Rough hands rip open my flannel, sending the buttons flying. His claw tipped fingers grazing my flesh have me tipping my head back, my loud cry echoing into the night air.

Above us, a full moon stares down from a velvet sky studded with a million stars. As I embrace my wild side, I wonder if I can ever go back to living in captivity again when his hot mouth claims my breast and draws my attention back to him.

Despite having shrunk back to his merely large size and looking more man than beast again, I still marvel at the differences between us. The texture of his white hair in my fingers is coarser than a human's and twice as thick. The smooth velvet of his skin is glorious under my fingertips, and as he bites my nipple and then swirls his tongue over it soothingly I can't help but be reminded of his sharp teeth.

One shove has my pants down, then he drops to his knees and fastens his mouth on my dripping core, pulling a volley of curses and gasps from my lips. The rapidly fading scientific part of my brain catalogs one more fabulous difference between us— that fucking tongue. Even with my legs trapped in my pants, he manages to snake it in one long lick from my back to my front.

My legs shake as he simultaneously pulses the base against my clit while the long tip works its way into my clenching opening. My desire drips down my thighs at the sensations that overtake me. This is yet one more thing that Ben had never wanted to do. So although my experience being on the receiving end of oral sex is pretty limited, I know there is no way this is humanly possible.

That knowledge coupled with the sensations has me climbing higher, cursing the pants tangled at my ankles that are preventing me from wrapping my legs around his head and riding his face. I groan in frustration which earns me a nip to my soft inner thigh.

I yelp in response, but he looks up at me, face shining with my arousal, and says, "What do you need, *Sruhnar?*"

I repeat the name back to him, questioning, "Sruhnar?"

He chuckles against me as he gently corrects my pronunciation, rolling the R softly. "My winter star."

I hold his face in my hands, staring down into his eyes, pupils blown wide reflecting the night sky above us. "And what do I call you?"

He looks away for a poignant beat and then meets my eyes again, almost shyly, and whispers, "Eryon."

I take care to pronounce it the same way, "Air-ee-on."

It flows off my tongue suiting the mythical creature before me. At the sound of his name on my lips, he rises to take my mouth in what starts as a soft, sweet kiss. As his hands sweep over my body, I can't help but wonder how long it's been since he has heard his own name. The loneliness and longing for a kindred spirit resonates within my soul and pours out through my kiss.

The simmering intensity shifts until I'm frantically kicking at my pants which are hopelessly tangled over my boots. Quietly chuckling at my huffs of annoyance, Eryon hoists me up. I let out a gasp as my back scrapes over the cold stone behind me, but it turns to a moan as he simply loops my legs behind his head and settles my weight over his shoulders.

I marvel at his strength, the power of his arms and shoulders rippling and flexing beneath me as he dives into my core, feasting on me with barely constrained hunger. His mouth boldly explores every inch of my skin, drawing moans from my lips and leaving me breathless.

My arms fling wide both in surrender and exhilaration, the precarious height below me adding a delicious edge of fear to my pleasure. I know he won't drop me, and despite being anything but petite, he holds me like I weigh nothing.

When his long, thick tongue spears into my entrance, I cry out. Being surrounded by nature as the guardian of the forest itself gorges himself on the arousal dripping from my core wrenches a rolling orgasm from deep within my belly.

My thighs shake and toes curl as I ride wave after wave. When I can't take any more I bury my hands deep into his hair and try to wrench his face away from me. I'm met with a fearsome growl and may as well have tried to push away the stone behind me, as unyielding as Eryon is.

With wide eyes I look down to where he continues to lap at my pussy. The sight of his tongue disappearing inside of me is so erotic and wickedly taboo I can't help but stare. Another gush of arousal pulls a deep guttural moan from him, vibrating against my flesh. Watching his sharp teeth graze my skin as he devours me has me grinding my hips harder into his face.

With his large calloused hands, he shifts his hold to my thighs and spreads me open even further. Never breaking our stare, he uses his long tongue to snake back to my ass, the probing lighting up erotic nerves I didn't know existed.

When his tongue breaches me, I can't help the squeal that escapes. I know it should be in shock, in reproach, but instead it turns into a deep moan as pleasure blooms within me. My pussy clenches at the emptiness, aching to be filled.

He buries his nose into my entrance, face flush with my body so my clit can grind into his forehead. The motion allows his tongue to slip further into my ass. I am so consumed with pure animalistic lust, I would have ground my flesh into the mountain itself at this point and not given a damn.

The sensations pulse and swirl together until a sudden deep pressure builds. He groans deep into me as I cry out and the vibration pushes me over the edge. As I feel myself coming, the pressure culminates in a gush of wetness shooting out of my sopping pussy, drenching his face.

"I—I'm so sorry," I stammer out, mortified that not only did I just squirt for the first time ever, but I did it directly into his face.

Eryon pulls back to look at me. But instead of the disgust I expect to see, he tips his head back and groans a deep guttural sound. He lets my body slide down the wall so I am pinned between him and the mountain, legs still tangled in my pants looped around his body.

Meeting my eyes, he flashes me a wicked smile, more teeth than lips, and says slowly, "You marked me."

"I know, I'm so sorry," I whisper from behind my hands as I hide, cheeks flaming with embarrassment.

He shoves them away to stare into my face. He drags a hand down his, scooping up the wet mess. He looks from his hand, dripping with my juices, back to me and then slowly and purposefully rubs it down his neck, over his chest, down those damn abs, and wraps it around his massive erection.

Face ecstatic, eyes unfocused, he repeats the process a few more times, spreading the liquid down over his velvet skin to the very tip of his cock. I watch in fascination, following the path of his hand over every rippling muscle and very closely as he coats his epic dick. It grows before my eyes, pulsing with engorged veins until I can feel the heat radiating off his body.

"My turn," he says darkly.

Reaching behind him, he shreds my pants, freeing my legs and claiming my lips in a brutal kiss. I can taste my orgasm lingering on his lips and tongue. I thought we had kissed before, but I realize, *this* is what a kiss with him is really like.

He explores every inch of my mouth, licking up into my palate, sucking my lips into his mouth, savoring every texture and contour. Emboldened, I lick into his mouth, running my much smaller tongue along his silky lips and the tips of his sharp teeth. I can only explore a fraction, but everything in my reach is fair game.

He pushes me to my knees, breaking the kiss. Squatting down to bring his cock in front of me, he starts rubbing himself all over my face. Guiding my head with a large palm cupping the back, he drags his soft skin and short white curls all over my face and neck.

Desperate for a taste I dart out my tongue as he moves my mouth under his large balls. I suck the barest tip of one into my mouth, moaning as his flavor explodes on my tongue. He tastes like the forest at night—dark, forbidden, dangerous. I can't get enough.

After he has coated me in his scent, he finally gives me the freedom to move my face where I want. I greedily wrap my mouth around the tip of his cock as it strains towards me. I lap and suck at it, wondering how I will be able to fit him into my body when I can hardly fit him into my mouth.

I wrap both hands around his girth and begin to work his length, twisting up and down, moving my hands in tandem. He drops his head back between his shoulders, panting and grunting out in a guttural language I'm unfamiliar with despite my time here.

I work up enough saliva that I can squeeze the tapered head of his cock into my mouth. When I do, I'm rewarded with the salty taste of his precum. The slippery liquid allows me to fit more of him in. I get a rhythm down with my mouth and hands, rewarded by groans and grunts as every muscle bunches with his restraint.

Heat radiates off him, and as I imagine being filled with his huge hot cock, I moan around him. He loses control, and grips my head in both hands to hold me steady while he thrusts his hips. I relax as much as possible, taking short panting breaths through my nose. As he feeds me his cock inch by inch, I relax my throat, and soon I'm taking more of him than I ever thought possible.

His cock stiffens, radiating heat like a furnace, and just when I brace myself to attempt not to drown in his cum, he pulls out of my mouth, saliva stringing between us. He wraps a large hand around himself and smiles down at me. Feeling confident at the look I put on his face, I tilt my face up to his, open my mouth, and stick out my tongue.

As I hoped, it's his undoing. His smile turns feral as he fists his cock with long, punishing strokes and comes with a roar. I had been expecting a lot, but nothing could have prepared me for the long ropes that shoot out to cover not just my face and mouth, but coat my breasts and body.

I look down at the copious streams, steaming in the night air, as they drip down. He gives himself one more pump, catching the last spurt in his large hand. Reaching out he uses it to smooth my tangled hair back from my face, dragging his hand along my jawline and swiping his thumb over my tongue as I kneel there, motionless in my surprise.

He repeats the same motions he had used on himself earlier, wiping the fluids over each breast, down my belly, through my trimmed curls, and down into my sex where he thrusts a large finger into me.

As he sweeps me up off my feet and into a scorching kiss, mingling our tastes, I can't help the small worry in the back of my mind that we just completed some type of marking ritual that I don't know the repercussions of.

CHAPTER ELEVEN

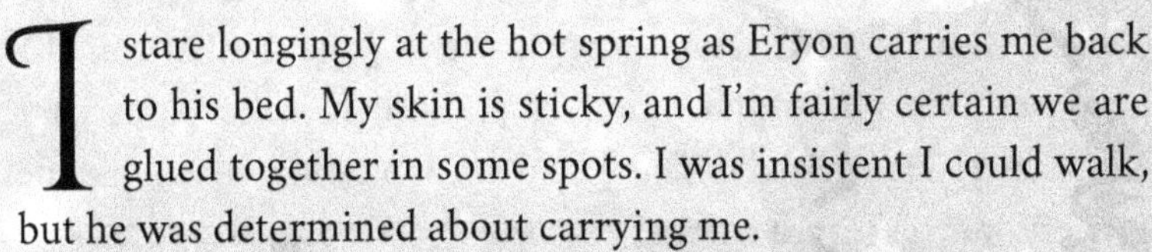

I stare longingly at the hot spring as Eryon carries me back to his bed. My skin is sticky, and I'm fairly certain we are glued together in some spots. I was insistent I could walk, but he was determined about carrying me.

I wonder what is in the sack he had retrieved from where the man in the woods had tossed it earlier, hoping it's food. My stomach lets out a loud growl in agreement. He playfully tosses me on the bed, and I let out a laugh.

As he stokes the fire, I watch the embers drift up with the woodsmoke and out the small hole in the very top of this particular cavern that seems to be his bedroom. I'm amazed at how comfortably he lives in such a primitive set up.

He dumps out the bag to reveal several fat silver fish. I'm thrilled to see them since we have been living on a plant based diet. It reminds me to ask, "Do you eat meat?"

"Rarely," he replies. "I will tonight, rather than waste them as they've already given their lives. But I am the guardian of the forest. I can easily survive without killing those under my protection."

Running my hands through the soft furs on the bed, I ask, "What about these?"

"I will take the pelts of animals that have fallen, that they may continue to have purpose. Sometimes things are given to me in offering."

"Like when you help people?" I ask, remembering Sita's story of the time her family had been saved from freezing by the Migoi bringing firewood. Though I hadn't believed it when she told me, now I know it was true.

He throws me a half smile and admits, "When they deserve it. But my first responsibility is the earth and its creatures."

I walk over to sit next to him as he roasts the fish over the fire. He hands me steaming bits, and I burn my fingertips and the roof of my mouth in my haste.

He smiles warmly at me as he passes me a waterskin. The simple dinner is delicious and made all the better for the company. We talk about our lives and laugh at how different they are. I'm surprised, and tell him so, about how up to date he is on modern life and current events.

He rolls his eyes at me as he explains he hears travellers talk and has even seen television through people's windows, which he assures me is the biggest waste of time he has ever witnessed.

I laugh and try to explain the plots of some of my favorite

shows and movies to him but even I have to admit, they seem inconsequential when I try to put them into words. My life seems like another world entirely sitting here in the cave next to him. One that I'm not sure I want to go back to.

"I'll show you something worth watching," he says, tugging me away from the fire by the hand after we finish eating.

He leads me through another series of branching tunnels until we emerge out into a veritable oasis. I look around in wonder at the lush plants surrounding us as the warm air wraps around my skin.

The mountains curve inward, forming a hidden basin where a rare microclimate blooms. Sheer cliff walls rise on all sides, arching toward each other to create a natural dome. Their jagged edges part at the top, revealing a skylight of shimmering stars.

I throw my arms wide and spin in a slow circle, taking in the beauty around me.

Eryon sweeps me up and spins me, a delighted smile on his face. Shyly he asks, "Do you like it?"

"Like it? I love it! Eryon, it's magical. What is this place?" I ask, breathless as he sets me back down on my feet.

"A sacred place. I've never brought a human here before. This is the heart of the mountain," he explains as he leads me to the center where a hot spring bubbles up.

Under the light of the moon, I can make out where rocks have been fit together to form a pool. I realize the heat of the thermal spring is trapped within the cliff walls to create this space. The botanist in me longs to return during the day to study the unique plants that must thrive here. The ethnobotanist in me wants to know how the people of the region have used these plants. Did they have access to them or had this miniature world remained a hidden secret? Did the Migoi use the plants here?

But right now, everything is awash in silver and grey under

the night sky in a beautiful monochromatic painting. As I turn back to face Eryon and see the stars reflected in his eyes, I feel something take root in my chest. My breath catches as I see the same feelings mirrored back to me.

I try to push it down, try not to let it bloom like the lush foliage around me. Because as beautiful as this place is, I know I can't stay here. No matter how much I want to. Not only can I *not* fall in love with a Yeti, but if I don't somehow find my way back to town and finish out my expedition, I'll die.

The inborn error of metabolism that claimed my mother's life will claim mine, too. The *Silene vitalis* carries the precise enzyme my body lacks, the key to breaking down the protein slowly poisoning me. I need the next few years to extract it and perfect the delivery mechanism in order to save myself, and others like me. And I won't discover it hiding away in a cave with a Yeti.

Tomorrow I'll ask him to bring me back to town—before these feelings can blossom. Although I think it might already be too late.

I let him lead me into the steaming water, gingerly lowering my body into the inviting heat. The stones are smooth below my feet as I make my way to the built-in stone bench. He pulls me against his chest, and we recline in the gentle current, watching the stars cross the sky above us.

"You're right. I've never seen a better show than this," I whisper.

His soft laugh rumbles beneath my ear. He reaches over and snags something off a plant, then leathers it up between his hands.

"Oh, a soapberry!" I exclaim, excited to have one of my questions answered. The Migoi do use the plants here.

I groan as he massages my scalp with his strong fingers, thankful to finally be washing away the marking from earlier. It had been hot at the time, but I was tired of the sticky dried patches. He seemed to suffer no such qualms, happily sporting spiky spots of clumped fur.

I reach for the soapberry and then stand on the bench behind him to return the favor. As I lather the soap and wash him, I marvel at the way his body changes with weather or under threat. How his size and shape can morph as needed, even his body temperature.

In the warmth of the pool, his skin is almost slick. As I run my soapy hands over his neck and shoulders, kneading the tight muscles, I realize this is the closest I have seen his flesh to my own. He could almost pass for human right now. A very, very large human.

Or maybe that is just my secret wish, that he could be a human and we could be together outside this cave system. But his size would never allow him to blend in, and one look at his luminous eyes and slightly too large teeth would give him away. He's just not quite human enough.

He melts into my touch as I massage down his back. With a groan he snags me with one massive hand and brings me to stand in front of him again. Taking the soapberry back from me he lathers it between his hands, staring into my eyes as he runs them up and down my body.

My skin flushes under his attention, the slippery glide of his fingertips lighting up my nerves as they slide up and over my breasts, then back down along the curve of my belly. With each pass, he brings his hands lower until I spread my legs in anticipation, desperate for him to touch my aching center.

I thrust my breasts into his hands, my breath catching every time he almost gets to where I need his touch the most, only to bring his hands back up to pull at my pebbled nipples again.

Frustrated, I reach out to grab his hands, but he pulls me into him with a chuckle. He brings his mouth to my ear and whispers, "My greedy winter star. Let me show you again. Let me show you are worth saving."

I nod, willing to agree to anything just to get him to touch me. He tugs me deeper into the pool. The moon has passed over the natural skylight of the basin, dropping us into darkness with only the pinprick of stars visible in the night sky.

"It's dark here," I whisper shakily, the memory of the avalanche's crushing blackness closing in on me.

"It is never dark where you are," he whispers fiercely, his voice a lifeline. "You *are* the light."

The earlier feeling in my chest blooms despite my best effort to keep it from flowering. I can't stop the tendrils of love from growing, even knowing that tomorrow I have to end this. I need to leave. But I deserve one night, I tell myself—just one night.

"Show me," I say with my lips, but what my heart says is, "You're my light, too."

CHAPTER TWELVE

He leads me to the far side of the pool under a thick canopy of foliage. He sits me on top of a large, flat rock and then pushes me back so that I'm lying down.

I tilt my head back to keep my nose and mouth just above the surface, letting the hot water cascade over my eyes and ears. The current surrounds me, caressing my arms and legs, while my breasts peek out into the air. Cut off from the world, all I can hear is my own heartbeat and the quiet whoosh of air in and out of my lungs.

My heart rate ticks up as I remember being caught in the cold, dark of the avalanche. I keep reminding myself I am warm, I am safe, and Eryon will protect me, yet again. As he trickles warm water over my peaked nipples, I let out a gasp, repositioning my head to keep my airway clear of the spring.

Over and over, the hot water trails over my flesh, alternating with his hands pinching and rolling my nipples. Not being able to see or hear when or which sensation will come next only heightens my pleasure. Anticipation of whether it will be the water or his hands builds, only to be surprised when a hot mouth seals around my breast, sucking and nipping.

Back and forth, he lavishes each breast with attention, one and then the other. My thighs part, wishing there was the strong current here like the other pool. Needy moans fall from my lips as my breasts become overly sensitized.

Then nothing is touching me, and I so desperately want to sit up, open my eyes and search for Eryon, but I remain motionless and count my breaths, now harsh even with my ears below the water.

Not a ripple in the water alerts me, and a startled moan escapes my lips as just a long, hot, wet tongue meets my clit. Just the tip, featherlight, swirls and flicks over and around my sensitive flesh, then snakes down and circles my entrance until I'm writhing, desperate for more. One large finger thrusts into me, and my breaths turn to pants as he expertly licks me, driving his finger in and out of my core. But it's still not enough.

"More," I pant out, wanting to be filled by him, my voice echoing in my head with my ears below the water's surface.

He laughs, the deep vibrations rolling through me as he pushes another thick finger inside of me. My pussy flutters around him, pulling him deeper. He curls them forward and stars flash behind my closed lids.

Keeping my nose and mouth above the water as my hips thrust against his hand is becoming almost impossible. When another finger probes my ass I know I am going to drown, albeit a very happy woman.

The intense sensation of being filled coupled with his swirling thick tongue has pleasure building inside of me. The pressure increases as he drags his tongue from my clit to work it inside of me alongside his fingers. The stretch is exquisite, but between my arousal and his wet tongue, it stays on this side of pleasure, riding the knife's edge of pain.

Further and further, his tongue pushes into me until the tip massages that spot from earlier inside of me. He brings his thumb up to strum over my clit, and the combination of the assault has me crashing into a white hot orgasm. I feel my pussy and ass spasming around his fingers and tongue. My hips grind down into him, desperate for more.

The water washes over my head, and I let it, abandoning all senses to focus solely on the ones between my legs. Sight, hearing, smell... hell, breathing doesn't matter when there is an explosion of emotion in my center.

It coalesces into one single point of nuclear heat and then explodes out like a supernova, igniting everything in its wake. My lungs are bursting, stars dance in my vision, and I don't want to come up for air because this is the best damn orgasm, the best *anything*, I've ever had in my life.

My limbs are getting heavy, and at any second I am going to drown. To surrender. But this will have been worth it. I drift in relaxed bliss and open my eyes, noting from somewhere far away how the stars ripple and shimmer from below the water's surface.

Eryon yanks me up out of the water just as I inhale, saving me from choking. Sweet air fills my lungs and, with it, frantic need. I want him. Now. I launch myself at him, surprising both of us, but he still catches me. He *always* catches me.

"Eryon, I need you," I pant out between frantic kisses.

He flips us so that he is sitting on the rock, the water lapping at his legs. He reaches to the plants at the shoreline and snags a leaf similar to an aloe plant, crushing it in his hand where it releases a gel-like substance. He strokes himself with it, covering his cock until it glistens.

Grabbing my hips, he brings me to straddle him, notching his head at my entrance. I ease down, hissing at the sting but pleasantly surprised as it fades. He reaches down to where we meet and slathers more of the gel over me.

"For the pain," he murmurs into my neck.

I slide myself down, working him into me by fractions. He stares into my face with a look of wonder, alternating with watching where he disappears into me.

"Look at you. I knew you could take me, Sruhnar. You are perfect. Divine. You were made for me," he says.

Arousal pools at his words, helping smooth the way to work more of him into my body. Between my own dripping pussy and whatever fantastic lubricating plant he used, he is slowly but steadily slipping into me.

Sweat blooms on my face, and I bite my lip at the tremendous effort it takes to fit his monster cock into me. He slathers more of the gel around his shaft and caresses my skin at our intersection. Bracing myself with my hands on his chest, I raise and lower my hips, each time I drop down, slowly advancing him inside of me.

"Open for me, my winter star. Take all of me," he growls. He wraps his hands around my hips, helping to support my weight but never pushing me faster, allowing me the time I need to adjust.

The stretch no longer stings, but instead fills me in a deeply satisfying way. I feel myself expanding to take him, proud of every inch I can get inside. I shift side to side, backwards and forwards, every pulsating vein, every ridge and contour sliding against my inner walls as he steadily advances.

I feel a surge of heat as his precum floods my core, and although I have taken as much of him as I can, I'm still inches away from being flush with his body. I can't help the sounds that fall from my lips, the cries and moans at the fullness.

He starts to thrust his hips up, small movements coupled with monitoring my expressions, but I only moan in pleasure as he continues to squeeze himself inside me, even past the point I thought I could take him. But he continues to disappear into me.

My thighs tremble, and he takes my weight completely with his grip, holding me steady as he slides his cock in and out. I let my head fall back between my shoulders, hands fisted in the hair of his chest.

When he takes my breast in his mouth, I snap my head back up to watch as he sucks almost the entire thing into his large mouth. He releases it with a pop only to repeat the process on the other side. The incredible sensation of suction and heat and grazing sharp teeth has me clenching around him.

"You are going to milk me with your tight heat," he groans, as he struggles to continue thrusting in and out of me with the increased tightness.

My head falls back again on a moan at his words, but he fists his hand in my hair and brings my ear to his lips. I gasp, spurring him to continue the onslaught of his gravelly voice into my ear.

"Is that what you want? To be stuffed full of my cock and then filled with my release? You want me to breed you? Fill you with my seed and keep you here with me? Take you everyday so deep and so hard, all you can think about is how this sweet, tight heat aches for me?"

At my moans and writhing he continues, voice even deeper,

"Or do you want to be marked by me again? Have me pull out and spill my seed all over your face and breasts? Rub it into your skin and claim you as mine?"

He reaches back to caress my ass again and continues, "Do you want me to claim *all* of you?"

I cry out, imagining what it would be like for him to take me where no one else has been. The stretch would be intense, but perhaps with the lubricating plant he could. I'd try anything with him. Everything.

"Eryon," I whimper, as his hips move faster while he holds me suspended above him, my belly bulging out with each thrust. "Yes. Fill me up. I need it. I want it."

He hauls me up to the edge of the pool, flipping us so I'm on my back with my legs wrapped around his hips. He grips my shoulders with his large hands, anchoring me, and begins thrusting, slamming his body into mine with long, brutal strokes.

I thought I had taken all of him into my body. I had been wrong. Very, very wrong.

He alternates his gaze from intensely staring into my eyes to looking down to where he disappears inside my body. He towers over me, blocking the night sky from my sight, but it doesn't matter, the only thing I want to see is him. I had been wrong earlier, this is the best show I've ever seen.

He pulls out to the tip and then slams back home. The heat, the velvet, the large pulsating veins slide against my inner walls over and over again. Nonstop cries fall from my lips as my heels dig into the soft fur along his flanks.

"Sruhnar, I can't hold out against your tight heat. Let me feel you. Now," he grinds out.

I can't help but respond to his command, my pussy rippling around him, milking his cock and pulling his seed deep inside of me just as he said. He roars his release and the thick ropes of heat painting my insides have pleasure rolling through me in waves as I clutch onto him, lost in the storm.

The long hard planes of his body, the slight velvet texture of his skin, the clear devotion in his eyes are the only thing anchoring me to the earth. Because…

I just mated with a Yeti, and it was fucking incredible.

CHAPTER THIRTEEN

Eryon pulls me close and sinks us back into the hot spring. The warmth of the pool washes over us. The sky above begins to blush with the first hues of dawn, dappled light filtering down to paint the scene in soft golds and pinks. His heartbeat thumps beneath my ear as I rest against his chest, and for a moment, I wonder if this is what paradise feels like.

My jaw-cracking yawn breaks the peaceful silence, pulling a laugh from both of us as he mirrors mine with one of his own. I promised myself today would be the day I left, but the pull of this place, and the weight of my exhaustion, make it impossible to go just yet.

First, I need sleep. And I don't know how I'm going to explain to Eryon that I need to go.

As he scoops me up bridal style, ignoring my insistence that I can walk yet again, I can't help but take in the local flora, now painted with the soft hues of breaking dawn. My gaze lingers on the plants clustered near the head of the spring, their delicate leaves and flowers catching the light. Something about them tugs at my memory, and a frown creases my brow as my sex-addled brain tries to figure out why this plant seems so familiar.

The heart-shaped leaves, the compact growth, the star-shaped flowers nodding gently on their bent stems—the golden light of dawn highlighting their iridescent petals which are the exact blue-violet of my eyes. My breath catches, and my heart stutters as the realization strikes with the force of the avalanche.

Silene vitalis. The name blooms in my mind, unbidden and impossible.

It's all I can do to weakly pat his arm in protest. He walks on, up and out of the water, passing by the plant without a second glance while I'm left grappling with the impossible truth it holds.

"Eryon, stop," I force out through the lump in my throat as I wriggle free from his grasp and slide to the ground.

Racing over to the plant, I collapse to my knees. With trembling fingers, I reach out and brush a leaf, and my breath catches. The key to everything I've searched for lies right here, within my reach. I never would have found it tucked away in this specialized microclimate. Never.

"Sruhnar," he calls sharply.

The edge in his voice makes me snap my head around. My heart stutters as I take in his expression. He storms toward me, his eyes flashing with anger, each step radiating a force I can feel through the ground beneath me. But all I can think about is my discovery. Nothing else matters at this moment.

"This is the plant I was looking for. This is the entire reason I came to the mountains." My voice cracks, a mixture of disbelief and relief flooding me. "I was going to have to leave to find it, but it's been right here the whole time. I'll need to take it with me."

Frustration gnaws at me as I think over the supplies I lack. Without my pack, I don't have what I need to preserve and transport the plant properly. I'll need a sterile setup, something to keep it cool and prevent the enzymes from breaking down while I figure out the extraction process. Maybe I should take a few plants, just to be safe.

I must have been mumbling my plan aloud to myself, the list of steps tumbling out under my breath, when Eryon interrupts me.

"No," he says flatly, his tone leaving no room for argument.

I glance up from the plant to meet his gaze. "No? What do you mean, no?"

He repeats it, more forcefully this time. "No."

Confusion and frustration bubble up inside me. "I don't understand. I just need a few plants for my research. Eryon, you have no idea how important this is. I can turn it into a medicine that could save lives. I *need* it."

His expression hardens, his voice carrying an edge of finality. "This plant has already cost lives. Nothing can leave this basin. I am its protector, and I will not allow humans to destroy my family again."

"What?" I gasp, stepping back, my confusion deepening. "Eryon, I thought you said you'd never brought a human here. What do you mean, 'destroy your family again'?"

I shrink back further as his body begins to grow, his form swelling with raw power until he towers over me, his presence suffocating when just moments ago it had been... everything. *We* had been everything.

"Humans," he snarls, his voice low and menacing. "They take and destroy, leaving nothing but devastation in their wake. Everywhere I go in the forest and the mountains, I see the damage they've caused. Plastic water bottles tossed into streams. The skies choked with haze. Forests full of ancient trees razed. Animals slaughtered for a few bites of meat, the rest of their bodies discarded as if their sacrifice meant nothing."

He starts to pace, his arms swinging wildly as his fury pours out. "Humans believe they have dominion over the earth and exercise their right to take and take without giving anything back, no matter the cost. I've witnessed their greed and devastation right here in this very spot. No, *I* didn't bring a human here to this sacred place."

He punctuates his statement by slamming a fist against his chest, then shakes his great head, as if in disbelief. "But my mate did. She brought a human here for that same flower. She was kind, always trying to help. Too trusting. He befriended her, gained her trust over time. The human told her he just needed one. Just one. Do you know how he repaid her trust? Do you know?"

His roar rips through the air, terrifying in its grief. The mountain shudders beneath me as if it quakes with his anger. His devastation. Even the plants tremble.

"He took the winter star. Not just one, but every single one he could find. She begged him not to, tried to explain that we needed it for our little snowling, who had fallen ill after the human's first visit. We didn't realize, until it was too late, that a simple human sneeze would cost us our child's life."

He pauses, his voice thick with emotion. "Yes, the winter star can save lives—ours and perhaps others. But it's also taken them, and I'm not willing to sacrifice any more for this plant."

He looks at me with cold fury, "Or for a human."

The weight of his words devastate me. I am just trying to save myself and anyone else with this same disease. But now I can't help but wonder what is the value of a life, human or otherwise? Is taking the plant worth his sacrifice? The plant, the research—is it worth all of this?

I remember the cave paintings—two Yetis, with a little furball nestled between them. My heart aches for Eryon and his family. The *Silene vitalis* had been cataloged and brought back to America nearly a century ago. Only my searches on plant genetics and mass spectrometry coupled with my research in ethnobotany had led me down a rabbit hole to this plant.

My last hope.

"What happened to your mate?" I whisper as tears streak my face. As hurt as I am, I still need to know the rest of his story. The exact price of this flower.

"She couldn't survive the loss of the snowling," he says, voice cracking in anguish.

"Eryon, I'm so sorry for your family. I'm sorry about what humans have done and still do. For all the destruction we cause. But you don't understand—I *need* this plant. This isn't about taking or destroying—it's about survival."

My voice cracks, and I take a shaky breath before continuing, "My life is at stake. Without the *Silene vitalis*, I won't make it. I know it's hard to trust humans, and I understand why you'd want to protect this place, this plant. But please, don't let my desperation make you think I'm like the ones who've hurt you."

"Leave," he growls, his eyes narrowing.

I slowly back away, struggling to my feet. "Leave?"

"This is the only reason you came here," he spits, throwing my words back at me. "You're no different from the others. You want to take it for yourself, and damn the consequences."

His chest heaves with anger, but there's something else—something raw beneath his words. *The only reason you came here,* echoes in my mind. I've reduced him, and whatever this is between us, to nothing more than a dalliance. A fun little side quest in my search for the plant. My heart cracks under the weight.

"It took me decades to get this plant to repopulate, from the single one that was left, a small seedling he missed. The only thing that kept me going, the only thing that gave me hope, was the possibility of someday having another snowling. I did this for them. For my family. For my future. And now—" His voice cracks, and he deflates, falling hard to his knees.

The weight of his grief hangs in the air, a reminder of the sacrifices he's made, and of what I'm threatening to take from him.

"Maybe you can still have a family, a snowling. I hope that for you, Eryon, I do. Not to replace the one you lost, but because I can see how important it is to you. I would never take all the plants. I would never try to hurt you," I say. Each word rings out with sincerity, but they fall hollow in the face of his grief.

"I've never seen another of my kind. I don't deserve another family after I failed to protect them. But I am the sworn protector of this place, of the forest and the mountains. And I will not allow you to destroy all I have left," he says.

"Eryon, I'll die without the plant," I say softly, my voice a whisper.

"Leave me here with my ghosts," he growls, his voice cold and final. "The world is vast, but this corner is mine. Go find something else. I won't be used, not again."

I stagger back, as if struck by a blow. I never planned on using him. I didn't deceive him. This was all an incredible, inexplicable coincidence. My chest throbs with the crushing weight of my failure.

Tears blur my vision as I stumble through the dark tunnels, the chill of the cave air seeping into my bones. Each step on the hard stone feels like a betrayal, the echoes of my feet reminding me of the warmth I once had in his arms. With every step, I am more acutely aware of how I am more alone now than ever.

At last, I reach the sleeping cave, the space feeling colder and emptier than before. I need clothes to leave this place in the dead of winter, but I have no idea where I am or how I can find my way back to town. I slump down next to the fire, staring into the glowing coals, casting around for a plan.

The sudden appearance of Eryon makes me jump. He throws my pack at my feet and coldly says, "Get dressed."

As I put my clothes on, I feel my wildness bleed away. I will be constrained by society, by my future, once again.

The tears drip steadily off my face until I'm snuffling. I cobble together an outfit from my pack, vaguely wondering how he found it. Pulling on my pants reminds me of when my old pair were looped around his body. Tying my boots with their mangled laces only reminds me of when he cut them off.

All the moments we shared, I thought they meant something. I foolishly thought I had been falling in love with a Yeti. Even stupider, I thought I was going to save my own life.

Instead, I will return home empty-handed again. To nothing. I have *nothing*.

I zip up my parka and shoulder my bag. The Migoi pulls it off my shoulders and throws it over one of his, the bright yellow pack looking comically small against him. He takes off, and I scramble to keep up with his long strides.

Before long, we emerge into the bright sunlight. I follow, squinting and struggling to keep my balance on the snowy path and match his pace. Every few minutes, I fall behind, and he stops to wait but never turns back to look at me.

We walk, and we walk. Finally, exhaustion takes over. My

heart heavy with grief, I trip and sit down hard. There, on the cold, unforgiving ground, I stay, lacking the strength to go on.

When he realizes I'm not following him, he returns. Our eyes meet in a hard stare. With a deep, frustrated sigh, he picks me up again. I don't want to sink into his warmth. I don't want to curl my fingers into his thick white fur. I don't want to remember how this felt when he saved me. In an ironic twist, he's carrying me to my death.

CHAPTER FOURTEEN

At some point I must have dozed off because, suddenly, the air is warmer and the forest is changing. I can feel the trees thinning around us, and the daylight is fading again. He must have carried me for hours.

The rushing of the river greets us as he sets me down on my feet and steps back. I look towards the sound to see if I can catch a glimpse of where we are, but when I turn back to ask him—he's gone. Disappeared without a trace back into the woods without a goodbye or even a "fuck off."

Some small part of me can't help but wonder if he ever existed at all. But the pain gripping my heart and soreness between my legs are visceral reminders of just how real he is.

I follow the sound of the rushing water, blinking back more tears, unsure how I have any left. I settle my pack more securely on my shoulders, freeing my hands to grip the rope railing of the precarious bridge that spans the river.

Once across, I climb up a small hill and get my bearings. A cold gust pushes me back towards Eryon, but it would take more than the north winds to bring us back together. I lean into it and head towards the familiar guest house that I spot just ahead. As if Eryon knew exactly where to bring me back to.

I slog my way through the snow and slush, and make my way over the stone path to find my door still locked with my own lock. I fish the key out of the side pocket of my pack and let myself in.

Everything is just as I left it. I drop my bag by the door and glance longingly at the bed. The idea of crawling under the thick quilt and letting heartbreak and exhaustion take over is almost irresistible.

But I owe it to Sita and Tenzig to check in, let them know I made it back safely, and ensure Sita did the same. With a final reluctant glance at the bed, I close the door behind me and head to the lobby to find my friends.

I let myself in and head straight for the fireplace, holding my hands out towards the welcoming heat. When they thaw, I spin around to warm my backside and barely have time to brace myself as Sita barrels into me, crushing me in a fierce hug.

She pulls back, hands on my shoulders, to study my face. "*Hai Migaia,* I can't believe you're alive. We looked for days but had given up hope of finding you!"

A trickle of guilt courses through me at the thought of my friends searching for me, believing me to be dead while I was busy getting busy with a Yeti.

"I'm so sorry, Sita! I can't imagine what that must have been like. I'm so happy to see that you made it back okay."

Tenzig brings us steaming mugs, and we all sit by the fire together. I sip the sweet chai, the liquid heat a comfort after the ordeals of the past few days.

"How did you survive?" Sita asks.

"I was able to get out of the avalanche and then I found a cave to rest in." The simplest explanation is usually the best. And I'm not lying, just leaving out key details.

She eyes me up and down, shaking her head in disbelief. "I know you'll find your plant now. The gods have surely smiled upon you."

I don't have the heart to tell her I did, only to lose it again. So instead I reply, "I don't know that the price is worth it anymore, Sita."

"What do you mean? You must find it! You'll die without it. Dahlia, your life is worth any price. And not just yours, this will help others, too," she says, concern and urgency coloring her words.

I place a gentle hand on her arm, my voice soft but firm as I say, "It's okay. I'll have to find another way."

She says, "I'm sorry, I don't blame you for not wanting to search the mountains anymore. Surviving an avalanche must have been traumatizing. Forgive me."

Now that I'm back, numbness is starting to creep in. I tell myself that I'm just exhausted and things will look better in the morning. But I can't help but think they won't. That, in fact, nothing will ever look better again.

After my third yawn, Tenzig bids me goodnight, and Sita insists on walking me back to my room. After she leaves, I stand by the window, staring across the river, straining my eyes to look for any movement in the dark woods beyond. Eryon hadn't even said goodbye, so I doubt that he would be out there, watching me.

The memory of his eyes, silver and luminous, flashes in my mind, as vivid as the first time I saw them on the edge of the forest I'm facing now. I ache to see them again, to know he's out there, that he hasn't truly disappeared from my life.

I stare into the night, unblinking, as if my will alone could bring him back so I could somehow explain not just why I need the plant but how I feel about him. But as the minutes stretch on, my eyes begin to water, and with the sting, I realize I'm staring at nothing but the same empty darkness that stands between us now. A great, gaping chasm.

Despite the ache in my heart, the scientist in me powers up my laptop so I can enter my notes. Now that I've finally seen the plant, I don't want to forget a single detail. The real life version matched the description I had found several years ago, but nothing could have explained the beauty of its luminescent blue-violet color.

Although now that I know how the specimen was originally obtained, I see its promise through a different lens. But tonight, my heart isn't in moving forward. I finish logging the details and then power down my computer, unable to make any decisions without sleep. Hoping things look clearer in the morning, I surrender to restless dreams of endless caverns and elusive silver eyes.

A FEW DAYS LATER, I wake to grey winter daylight streaming through the window and the sounds of voices. All I want to do is burrow under the covers, but before my eyes can close again, I bolt upright in bed.

Although it would be unusual for new travelers over winter, that isn't what is raising alarm bells. It's one voice in particular that shocks me to my core. I would know it anywhere after all these years.

"Ben," I hiss.

I crawl out of bed and quickly dress. Goosebumps that have nothing to do with the chill in the air cover my skin as I bundle up in warm clothes, hoping enough of me is covered that even if I do run into Ben, he won't recognize me.

I have to get to Sita and tell her that he can't know that I'm here and see if she can suss out just why the hell he is. Sita was wrong. The gods haven't smiled down on me.

I'm cursed.

Fuck my life, I think as I lace up my boots with their tattered laces that only serve to remind me of Eryon. I wrack my brain, trying to recall if I had told Ben the name of the guesthouse I was staying in. But I must have, because how else could he have found me?

Pulling my scarf up and my hood down to better hide my face, I ease the door open and peek out. The glare of the winter sun on the glistening snow has me squinting, but the coast is clear. I creep to the main lobby and quietly enter.

The air whooshes from my lungs on a startled gasp when I find Ben cozied up next to the fire, sipping a cup of tea. Like he's been waiting for me. Like he belongs here. Not a flicker of surprise even crosses his face. Instead, a satisfied smirk sits on his lips.

Shit, I was not expecting this. Despite me thinking he wouldn't recognize me all bundled up, I should have known better. His being at the same guesthouse is no coincidence.

I rip my hood back, pull down my scarf, and clip out, "Ben, what are you doing here?"

"Oh, Dolly. I've come to obtain the *Silene vitalis*," he sneers.

"Don't 'Dolly' me. I thought I made myself clear enough

when I broke your nose. I want nothing to do with you. And I don't need your help," I retort.

He lets out a humorless chuckle. "I didn't say I was going to help you. I said I was going to *obtain* it."

My mouth falls open as my mind churns, trying to piece together what he is saying. He's not here to help me, but he's here for the plant. Why?

"Well, good to see you, Dolly, but my crew is heading out now." He repeats the term of endearment with a sneer, just to needle me.

"You'll never find it," I say, lifting my chin in defiance.

"Lucky for me, you already did. And unlike your feeble attempt at a one-woman research expedition, I have the backing of not only the university, but a pharma company funding mine. Unlimited money and *manpower*. Turns out you stumbled on an enzyme they are very interested in. The drug they will develop will be worth millions. Maybe more."

"No," I cry, horrified by the thought of pharma sweeping through Eryon's caves, destroying his home, his paintings, the heart of the mountain where the *Silene vitalis* grows. I bite back my fear for my Yeti, but I can't help but say, "This area will be ruined. The people, the environment—"

He cuts me off and says, "You still don't get it, do you? You could have been something with my backing. Instead you're nothing but a stupid fucking girl chasing stories instead of science. You should have stuck to plain botany, no one cares about people or culture when there's money involved."

I stand frozen, shocked by the sudden turn of events. He knocks into my shoulder as he passes by, spinning me around to watch him leave.

He pauses at the door and throws over his shoulder, "I've told you before, you really should secure your files better."

I gape after him even after the door swings closed. My files. He was in my fucking files. This whole time, after being so dismissive of everything I had ever worked on, he had been keeping tabs on my work.

Of course he did. He had always fallen back on me "helping" him with his, both when he was getting his degrees and as a professor. When in actuality, everything had been my ideas, my research, my hard work and long nights. I'm not a stupid fucking girl. I was always the woman with the brains in this relationship. And I need to be the brains now.

"Think, Dahlia. Think!" I coach myself out loud. I try to remember what I had typed into my notes when I had returned. But I hadn't known where exactly the cave system was which means Ben doesn't know either.

If I can make it back to Eryon before Ben, I can warn him. I only hope he will listen to me after I'm the one responsible for bringing this threat to his doorstep. My heart breaks for him as the price of this plant just keeps getting steeper.

The sound of voices has me pressing my face to the window, trying to see what is going on without running into Ben and risking another confrontation. As I see his large, well-outfitted group heading out, I hold my breath, waiting to see what direction they head in.

To my relief, they don't head towards the river. As the last bright parka turns the corner, I burst out of the door and run to my room.

Once inside, I power up my computer. While it boots up, I grab some extra supplies and shove them into the top of my pack. I don't have time to take everything out and organize it and I have no idea what's still in there from my earlier trip. This will have to do.

I turn back to my laptop, planning to download my files and then wipe them from my online drive only to find I'm locked out of the University's system. I slam the lid closed, cursing, "Damn you, Ben!"

Swinging my pack onto my shoulders, I head out again, not

willing to waste a single moment. I have to get to Eryon first. Ben may have unlimited resources and *manpower*, but I have something on my side he'll never understand.

The sudden threat has made me realize I love Eryon, and I'm going to protect him. No matter the cost. He's paid enough. It's time for someone to show him that he is worth saving, too.

CHAPTER FIFTEEN

I glance around to make sure no one is in sight before sneaking back toward the bridge I crossed just yesterday. The river is swollen from the fresh snowfall, its roar filling the air as I grip the rope railings.

"Dahlia!"

I spin around, my heart leaping into my throat at the sudden sound of someone calling my name. Relief floods me when I see Sita.

"Sita! You scared me half to death!" I press a gloved hand to my chest, my heart pounding beneath my parka.

"I'm sorry! I didn't mean to," she says, breathless as she hurries to meet me. "I heard you and Ben. I had no idea who he was when he checked in. If I'd known, I would've come straight to you! Then I saw you leaving the guesthouse and knew something must be wrong for you to head back out so soon."

I sigh, guilt pressing down on me. "Sita, there's so much I haven't told you. But I don't have time to explain everything now. I need to find that cave I was in before Ben does."

She frowns, worry etched into her face. "Dahlia, it's dangerous to cross into those woods. The—"

I cut her off. "I know. The Migoi." I hesitate, knowing how absurd it will sound. "Sita, the Migoi—he's the one who saved me."

Her eyes widen, but I press on before she can speak. "And now, I need to save him. I found the plant in his cave, but Ben is here for it, too. We can't let him get there first."

Sita flips her hood up and pulls the zipper to her chin, determination bright in her eyes. With a sharp nod, she says, "Let's go. You can fill me in on the way. My family owes him a debt, too. I'll help you protect him as he has always protected us."

"I don't know where I'm going. He might be angry that I've brought danger to him, just as I'm bringing you into it. You don't have to come with me." The hope she'll back down and stay safe wars with the desire not to fight this battle alone.

She shakes her head firmly. "I think I know where to go. I've heard enough stories from travellers and passed down within my family about landmarks to reach his territory. And of course I have to go with you. What kind of friend would I be to let you face this alone? Besides, surely the Gods will smile upon us for honoring a dharma as sacred as protecting the protector."

"Right now, I need all the help I can get. I'd be foolish to refuse you. Thank you, Sita." My voice wavers as my eyes sting with unshed tears, moved by her loyalty. I was wrong. I don't have nothing. I have everything. Friendship, integrity, intelligence—and I'm in love with a Migoi.

I echo her phrasing, a small smile tugging at my lips despite the gravity of the situation. "Let's go protect the protector."

Taking a deep breath, I step onto the bridge, the ropes creaking under my hands as the icy wind whips around us and the river rages below. Sita follows close behind, as we retrace my earlier steps as far as I can remember.

We quickly exhaust the extent of my knowledge so Sita takes the lead. As we hike as fast as the trail and weather allow, she begins to recount the stories passed down through generations in her family and overheard snippets from the many travelers who have stayed at the guest house.

"My grandmother always said the Migoi are guardians of more than just the forests and mountains. They keep the balance between the human world and nature, between man's greed and earth's abundance. Let's follow the landmarks from the stories, and if they're right, we should end up at the caves."

Her voice carries conviction, each word pushing back against the cold and fatigue threatening to set in. It's enough to spark hope. Even with the wind biting at my face and the trail ahead uncertain, I can't help but think we might just make it.

HOURS LATER, doubt begins to creep in. The trail has become a monotonous cycle of cold and up. Ever upward. Our conversations have dwindled, replaced by the sound of heavy breathing, and our stops to rest are more frequent. We're both struggling to keep up the pace as we look for the first landmark, something about watchful eyes.

Darkness is falling fast, and when I stumble again, I call out, "Sita! We can't keep going like this. We won't be able to find these eyes in the dark, anyway."

She nods, gesturing to a rock face ahead. When we stop, it helps to block some of the wind, making me realize just how brutal the weather here is. Sita was right, this side of the river is completely different.

I drop my pack and stretch my tight shoulders. Sita pulls off hers and, with practiced ease, sets up a compact four-season tent. My spirits lift at the thought of even a little time out of the weather. I'm beyond grateful for her presence.

We crawl into the tent, and while I'm still partly frozen, the lack of wind chill inside is such a relief. Sita pulls out a small stove and starts heating water. She hands me a sleeping bag, then unrolls her own. I can't believe how poorly prepared I was for this journey. I really wouldn't have made it without her.

By the time our beds are set up, the water is hot. While she makes tea, I dig out the protein bars I had hurriedly thrown in the top of my pack. My fingers and toes tingle as they warm up, and my face feels like it's finally thawing. Our simple dinner tastes like a feast, and the hot tea fills me with warmth, rekindling my energy and hope.

Despite the physical exhaustion, I struggle to fall asleep. My mind keeps rehearsing what I'll say to Eryon if we find him. *When* we find him, I correct myself. Still, a part of me can't shake the worry that he won't listen—or worse, that he'll blame me for Ben's pursuit. And, honestly, I wouldn't blame him. After all, if he hadn't rescued me from that avalanche, none of this would have happened.

Although I regret the danger heading his way, I can't regret the time we spent together. It was cathartic, and I've come out of it stronger. Fiercer. Unlike Ben, who I sure as shit regret my time with. But all these experiences, whether full of pain or pleasure, have shaped me into who I am today. The old Dahlia never would've rushed off into the Himalayan mountains to save a Yeti. But the new Dahlia does.

Because I'm Dahilia fucking Wilde.

I must drift off because the next thing I know, Sita is shaking me awake. We quickly break camp, barely stopping for tea.

As we trudge up the mountain, the trail growing steeper with every passing step, the world becomes a blur of white snow, gray rock, and the relentless howl of the wind. Just when I think I can't go on, Sita stops.

"Didi, look!" she exclaims, pointing ahead. "The watching eyes. We need to pass through them."

I follow her gaze and see, partially uncovered by the shifting snow, two massive round boulders that form a narrow passage between them. A thrill runs through me at our luck.

As we walk through, I stop and turn back to look at the stones. The late sun strikes their surface, and that's when I see it. There's writing on the rock that looks like it was recently scratched into the surface.

"Sita, can you read that?" I point to the word.

Squinting at the mark, she mouths a few different possibilities before saying, "I don't know this language, but it looks close to some words I do recognize. If I'm reading it correctly, I think it starts with Sru—?"

My lips curve into a smile as my heart leaps. "Sruhnar."

She looks at me with wide eyes and then back to the carving, "Yes, that fits. But what is it?"

He carved my name into a rock. It's a gesture so simple, yet so profound—it must be the Migoi's way of marking our connection, like two lovers carving their initials into a tree. My spirits surge, and I'm suddenly re-energized. Without thinking, I break into a run, laughing, with Sita hot on my heels.

"My name," I call back over my shoulder.

Our pace slows with the fading light, and although we are

clearly making progress, neither of us have any idea how far we've come or how far we've yet to go. I hate to stop and make camp but the darkness leaves us no choice. And getting injured is not an option in the wilderness.

THIS MORNING, I'm the one waking Sita at first light. In wordless agreement, we pack up and break camp. We eat as we walk, even skipping tea in favor of hitting the trail. Today feels significant, and I can sense that whatever this journey holds, it's about to end.

Within a few hours, she points out another landmark. Jagged, snow-covered rocks frame the entrance like icy sentinels.

"The whispering gorge is the passageway to the Migoi's territory. After this, we only need to find the frozen falls which mark the entrance to the cave. Let's wrap our scarves around our ears and pull up our hoods—if the stories are true, it will be loud."

Her instructions sound strange, especially for something called the whispering gorge, but I follow her lead without hesitation. As I adjust my hood and scarf, a flash of red at the entrance catches my eye, a vivid shock of color against the muted landscape.

I jog over and kneel to brush away the snow and stones to pull it free. A laugh escapes me as recognition sparks in my chest at the scrap of lace.

"He's leaving me a trail," I murmur, more to myself than to Sita. The thought of him watching over me, guiding me, has tears pricking at my eyes.

She glances over, her brows lifting in curiosity. "The Migoi?"

I nod, holding up the scrap of fabric from my torn panties.

"He knows I'm coming for him. And if he's leaving clues..." my voice trails off, a flicker of excitement rising. "It's like he wants me to find him."

She tilts her head, considering, and then offers a faint smile. "Then let's not keep him waiting."

With renewed purpose, we enter the gorge, and the first freezing gust hits us like a slap in the face. It's not the whisper I'd imagined but a high-pitched primal scream that reverberates in my skull.

"Loud is an understatement," I manage to shout, my voice just audible over the noise.

Sita nods, her face half-hidden behind her scarf.

"Keep moving!" she calls, her words carried off almost as soon as she speaks.

Step by step, we fight through the chaos. The wind drowns out everything, while the cold bites at my exposed skin, and panic flutters at the edges of my mind in the consuming chaos.

I force myself to focus, closing my eyes for just a moment. I think of Eryon, of the heat in his touch and the sound of my own breath echoing in my ears under the water of the hot spring. I remember the cave where he stripped me of sight and sound, leaving only sensation and trust, helping to heal me from the ordeal of the avalanche.

The memories of the slide of his tongue against mine, the caress of his fingers, and the fullness of him inside me, proving to me that I am worth saving, spur me to push forward—it's my turn to show him that he's worth saving, too.

Slowly, the walls of the gorge widen, and the howling wind begins to fade. It's over. The stillness is deafening, almost surreal.

Sita turns to me and cheers triumphantly, "We did it!"

"When you tell this story," I say, exhaling a shaky laugh, "don't call it the 'whispering gorge.' Call it the buckle up buttercup this shit is loud gorge or something far more accurate."

Her smile widens, and she shakes her head. She replies with a wry tone, "Noted."

We press on, snow crunching beneath our boots and the fragile blossom of hope held in my heart.

CHAPTER SIXTEEN

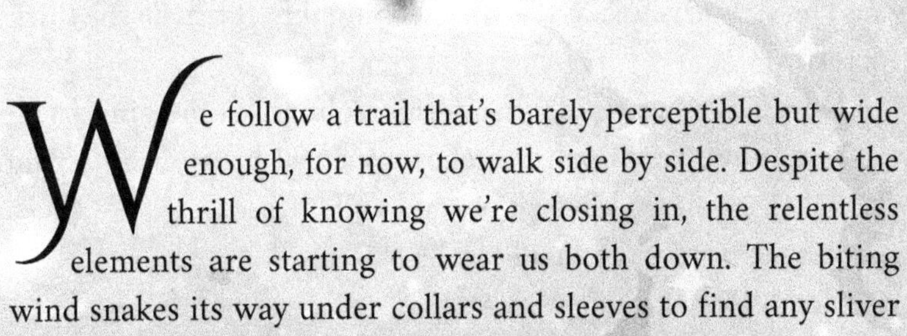

We follow a trail that's barely perceptible but wide enough, for now, to walk side by side. Despite the thrill of knowing we're closing in, the relentless elements are starting to wear us both down. The biting wind snakes its way under collars and sleeves to find any sliver of exposed skin, and my legs ache with every step.

Our pace has slowed, each movement feeling heavier than

the last. The short days of winter are against us, the dimming light urging us to hurry despite our exhaustion.

I don't know how many more days we can survive on little sleep, protein bars, tea, and sheer hope. Today has to be the day. It *will* be the day. There isn't any other choice.

We inch around a steep curve, the trail thinning until it's barely more than a jagged ledge clinging to the mountainside. A misstep here could send us plummeting into the abyss below.

My focus narrows to the extraordinary effort of sliding one foot forward, planting it with care, then dragging the other to meet it. Above us, snow begins to flurry down, dusting our shoulders and obscuring the already treacherous path.

Just when I think the rest of my existence will be nothing but cold, gray trudging, Sita lets out a sudden whoop of excitement. I force my tired legs to shuffle faster and round the final bend, breath catching at the sight before me.

She stands, grinning at an enormous pillar of ice in a small clearing.

"The frozen waterfall," I exhale, my voice hardly more than a whisper.

We drop our packs and approach together, necks craning to follow the frozen wonder as it arcs skyward. The blue ice glimmers in the fading light, every jagged edge and smooth plane refracting a spectrum of color. I can't resist placing my gloved hand on it, marveling at the chill seeping through even the thick material.

As my gaze drifts down the icy column, something small wedged into a tiny fissure catches my eye. I brush it free from the light dusting of falling snow and pull it free.

Sita peers over my shoulder. "Is that a—"

"Soapberry," I finish with a smile.

For a moment, the cold and hardship melt away replaced by warmth flooding through my veins. We made it. But our victory is short lived, as the sound of slow clapping shatters the burst of happiness. I whirl to find Ben, flanked by his team and a man holding a familiar snarling wolf, straining against its leash.

"They must have paid him well," Sita says, her voice taut with anger at seeing a local guide with Ben's group.

I nod grimly, my hand tightening around the soapberry. "Well enough for him to risk the Migoi's wrath—especially since, to him, he's no myth. We had a run in with this guy before."

Sita's voice cuts through the tension, seething with a fury that matches the storm that has started raging around us, as if even the mountains are angry. She calls out, "How could you betray the Migoi who has guarded these mountains for centuries? To turn against him is to break your dharma and dishonor the balance of nature."

"Greed," I say, my voice cold as I pass judgement on the group in front of us. All guilty of the same sin.

My poor Eryon. Why must this be the price he pays over and over? Why is this his reward for centuries of watching over the mountains and forests, helping wherever he could? Another evil man coming to take what he has painstakingly recultivated?

Rage bubbles up inside me, scorching and relentless. I came here to show Eryon that he is worth saving too. And damn it, I'm going to do just that.

"Ben," I call out, extending my hand toward him in a placating gesture. "I guess it's my downfall, too. You're right. There's no way I can finish this without you. Can you at least get me back into the University? I know how much pull you have there."

I take a few hesitant steps and say, "I'll help you get the plant, but I need access to the future drug—and something to go home to. I know you could never forgive me, and I'm not asking you to. But please, throw me a bone here."

Years of being with this narcissist have taught me how to play him like a fiddle. Pander to his pride, stroke his ego, make him feel like the big man who's doing a favor for poor, helpless Dahlia.

Sita stands frozen, her eyes wide in disbelief at my sudden change of heart. I have to trust that she will sense my plan and not give me away.

I turn to her, pretend to dig in the pocket of my parka, and then place the soapberry in her hand. "Here, you might as well take the key to my room back since I won't be needing it anymore."

She cocks her head at me, brows furrowing in confusion as she looks down at what I've pressed into her hand. She hardens her voice and says, "I don't want you back anyway if you're going to join these men."

I feel her fingers curl around mine, a subtle but telling signal that she understands.

"Oh, Dahlia," Ben croons. "You always were a stupid girl. The men are already here. I don't need you. And I don't want you."

He lets out a cruel laugh, but I lean into my facade and push the farce further.

"Ben," I cry, pretending to be heartbroken. "You still need to navigate the cave system. You have no idea what that beast is like. I can help you."

His eyes narrow as he considers my words. Thankfully, all of my field notes were strictly professional, no mention of my relationship with the Yeti, so as far as he knows, what I'm saying is true.

I hesitate, not wanting to overplay my hand but knowing I'm running out of time. I need him impulsive, not analytical. "Ben, I barely escaped with my life. Please, let me help you. I just want to make sure this plant gets turned into medicine. I am the one who needs it because I inherited the gene. You have the power to save my life."

A smile spreads across his face at the crack in my voice, at my desperate plea. I didn't need to act that last part out. It's my truth.

His chest swells with self-importance, and I see the gloating aura settle around him. "Dahlia, you know I'm a good man. Of course, I'll save your life. The headlines will be incredible. Hell, the PR story will have investors scrambling to fast-track this drug and my payout. Fine. You lead the way. But make no mistake—I won't hesitate to kill you. This plant is worth more to me than your life."

"Of course, Ben. Thank you," I say, eyes downcast to hide the victory that must be shining in them.

An inhuman roar echoes, small stones tumbling down the rock walls surrounding us. Ben's team exchanges worried glances as the man with the wolf backs away, wisely disappearing.

The remaining men close ranks, flanking Ben. When their eyes go round, I don't need to turn around to know Eryon is behind me. The very air shimmers with his presence, menace and danger radiating off him in waves to collide against my back.

My lizard brain screams at me to run. Fear licks through my veins like fire and pools low in my belly, bleeding into desire that pulses in my core as I recall the feel of him against my skin, the heat, the lust. To be this close to him again yet so far away is excruciating. I don't ever want to be apart from him again.

"Sruhnar," he growls.

I spin to face him, dragging my gaze up his terrifying form, awed at his presence even after we had explored every inch of each other's bodies. He appears larger and more fearsome than ever. Chest heaving, luminous silver eyes snapping with ice cold fire.

When our eyes meet, I see his filled with exquisite pain and realize he must have heard my ruse.

"Er—" I start, but he cuts me off.

"Do *not* say my name," he snarls at me, lip curling to reveal his sharp teeth.

"He told you his name?" Sita asks, shocked into speaking.

When I glance at her questioningly, she whispers, "Migoi only tell their mates their names. They have great power. In all the centuries this Migoi has been here, no one knows his name. Except you."

Her words knock the wind from my lungs. I fell in love with a Yeti. And it sounds like he had loved me, too. If the rage bleeding off him is anything to go by, I think he still does. I know he watched our journey here, leaving me breadcrumbs along the trail.

Now it's my turn to be the white knight. I'll save the day, and then I can explain my subterfuge and we can forget about the rest of the world. Even if staying here with him means my death, I'd rather die by his side than live without him. Being devoured by him, filled with his heat hidden away in the caves sounds like a fine way to pass whatever remaining time I have left.

I would finally be living for myself—on my terms, driven by my own goals and ambitions. If love is the sum of those things, then so be it. I deserve it. I deserve *Eryon*. His name thrums through my veins like a mantra, fueling me with a fierce determination. My gaze snaps back to him, trying to communicate with my eyes my true intentions.

I try to piece together a solution, shifting the invisible chessboard in my mind, searching for the elusive strategy that will save us. But the odds are daunting. Ahead of me stands one very enraged Yeti, and behind me looms one very dangerous man. The space between them feels like a no-man's-land, and I am the one caught in the crossfire.

A loud click breaks the silence, and I spin back to Ben to see him holding a gun, aimed straight at Eryon.

"I can't imagine what the payout will be for this monster

plus the plant. You won't be so fierce when you're locked in a cage, *snowman*," Ben sneers.

I don't think, I just react.

Time plays out in slow motion as my boots dig deep through the layer of freshly fallen snow and crunch down into the gravel, propelling me towards Ben until I am launching myself at the outstretched weapon in a desperate attempt to shield my love. I'm already marked for death. Let Eryon have a second chance.

Above the pounding of my heart, I hear Sita scream as the gun recoils in Ben's hand. I should be scared, terrified of being shot but instead, all I feel is a deep sense of calm in achieving what I had set out to do. For even if I die, Eryon will know that he is worth saving.

As something pierces my shoulder, time resumes its normal pace. I brace myself for excruciating pain and reach up to grab my shoulder. I pull my hand away expecting to see blood from a gunshot but instead, I pull out a dart. I try to bring it up to my face for a closer look but my arm falls limply to my side.

Sticky syrup floods my veins. My legs buckle, and I land hard on my knees, then fall to my side. I am completely paralyzed, helpless to do anything except watch the drama unfold around me.

For a second Ben looks shocked, almost as if he can't believe he shot me. As if maybe, at one point, he really did love me.

"You're the only monster here, Ben," I want to scream, but I can barely force the whispered words past my lips as the fast-acting sedative courses through my body.

Fierce determination crosses his face, erasing any semblance of a human with feelings or morals, as he grabs for another dart. Before he can reload, the Yeti is on them. I watch in deep satisfaction as Eryon goes feral, swiping at the men with his great arms and knocking them over like bowling pins.

Red splatters the ground and the thick pelt of the Migoi, a

startling contrast against a world of white. He picks each man up, breaking them like kindling and tossing them over the edge of the trail, down into the abyss.

Except for Ben, crawling away on all fours like the coward that he is. Eryon swipes him up but doesn't kill him right away. Instead, he takes him in his massive hands, hoisting him into the air as if he weighs nothing. For a terrifying moment, the Yeti holds him there, staring deep into Ben's eyes.

Then Eryon shatters the silence with a fierce roar, the sound ricocheting off the mountains and rumbling through the earth itself. The air vibrates with its fury, dislodging loose rocks to cascade down the jagged walls like rain.

Ben's eyes go wide, the whites showing all around in a mask of terror. Without warning, the Migoi hurls him skyward, flinging him out into the abyss. His screams stretch out, growing fainter as he plummets into nothingness, the echoes haunting the mountain long after he's vanished from sight.

I desperately want to move, to run to Eryon and reassure myself that he is okay. Tell him I love him and I am so, so sorry. But not only am I paralyzed, I feel my heart slowing, my breathing softening in reaction to a sedative dose for something much larger than me.

I give myself over to this soft world. At least I'll die with the satisfaction that Ben got exactly what he deserved. I just wish I had the chance to tell Eryon that I love him.

CHAPTER SEVENTEEN

Time passes by in a series of polaroid pictures. Snapshots of light and movement, worried faces, being enveloped in heat and soft fur, the most delicious thing I've ever tasted poured into my mouth, and then—nothing.

Perhaps this is what death is. Simply nothing. If I'm dead, I may as well catch up on my rest without the wind howling and the cold scrabbling at me like skeleton's fingers. Although I doubt I would need sleep if I'm dead so that must mean…

I'm alive.

My eyes snap open on a sharp inhale, the smell of deep earth warm and familiar. A faint undercurrent of snow and pine tears at my heart. My Yeti.

I stretch like a cat, and the furs piled on me fall as I sit up to find myself naked. I reach up to my shoulder and explore with my fingertips, searching for any damage from my run in with the tranquilizer dart.

My skin is smooth and unblemished, not so much as a pinprick or even a bruise to mark where Ben shot me. In fact, as I swing my legs over the edge of the bed, I notice it—I feel amazing.

Carefully I stand, but my legs are sturdy and strong. I listen for the presence of anyone else, but all I hear is the quiet sound of the cave breathing.

Spying my pack leaning against the wall, I grab it and bring it next to the fire. Unable to recall the last time I ate, I root around, looking for a snack. Frustrated when I can't find something quickly, I decide to dump the contents out.

As I dig to the bottom of the upended pile, my fingers brush something unfamiliar—a bundle of moss and bark, wrapped and bound with delicate vine. I didn't pack this.

My breath hitches, confusion giving way to realization as I carefully open it. Inside, nestled with such care it nearly breaks my heart, is the *Silene vitalis*. Its petals are pristine, shimmering faintly even in the dim light of the fire's coals.

He gave it to me. A whole intact plant, roots and all. Lovingly packed.

Eryon cast me out, heartbroken over the old traumas and fears of being used and duped. Yet he did this—ensured I would live, even if we'd never see each other again. A lump forms in my throat, hot and suffocating, as I clutch the bundle to my chest.

He saved me, even when he was worried the cost had been too high. Ben said my life was worth nothing to him, despite all the years I had devoted to him. But Eryon showed me, with this one gesture, that my life means everything. That I was worth saving, yet again.

Cradling the precious gift to my heart, I race out into the cave system looking for him. I want to call out his name but hesitate after he told me not to. As I run, I ponder Sita's words. Since he told me his name, does that mean I am his mate? Do I want to be?

My feet carry me straight to the home of the *Silene vitalis*, like an invisible string is pulling me to my Migoi. I'm amazed by my speed. My lungs easily handle the increased demand for oxygen, and my heart rate barely accelerates as I fly towards him.

I burst out into the magical alcove, met by the lush landscape and mineral scent of the hot springs. My eyes are drawn to the great skylight above showcasing the tapestry of a million stars cast upon a midnight velvet sky.

Walking to the base of the spring, I gently replant the luminescent blue-violet flower near its brethren. The earth is soft and fragrant under my hands as I arrange the fragile roots, nestling them into the soil and then covering them lightly.

I take a step back, smiling proudly at the way the plant looks like it had never been disturbed. Sure, the plants are promising, but here is where they belong. Not in a lab, stolen from their home and protector.

A wall of heat crashes into my back, and I know Eryon is standing behind me. I am both dreading and anticipating this moment in equal parts. Does he understand why I said what I did? Does he still care for me?

Before I can weigh the thoughts, he whispers my name, *his* name for me, "Sruhnar."

The way he rolls the R reverberates deep in my belly as I turn to face him. He is standing so close I could reach out and touch him, can feel his breath coasting over my flesh, smell the crisp scent of snow and pine that clings to him.

My lips part on my inhale, trying to breathe in his very essence. I want to explain every moment, clarify every word that he witnessed, but he doesn't allow me the chance. Instead, he sweeps me up into his great arms and molds me to his body, claiming my lips in a hungry kiss.

I pour my explanation, my apology, my hopes and desires into every touch of our lips which says more than my mere words ever could. My legs wrap around him as my hands sink deep into the thick fur across his chest, my fingertips seeking the unique velvet texture of his skin.

His scorching kiss tells me that all is forgiven. Balance has been restored.

"Mate me," I gasp out between kisses. "I want you to mate with me at your wildest. I am not afraid. I want all of you."

"I will be more beast than man. It will be raw, primal. This will not be any gentle lovemaking, no plant to ease the way. It *will* be a claiming. And once I claim you, I cannot, *will not*, let you go," he declares.

I square my shoulders and meet his eyes, my voice firm as I say, "I don't want you to let me go. I want to claim you just as much as you want to claim me. I don't care what you are, as long as you are mine."

A wicked smile stretches across his lips and challenge dances in his eyes. He pushes me off him and starts backing away. Yet instead of shrinking with the distance, his form grows and grows. His long white hair lengthens and his muscles flex. Even his canines appear more prominent.

The transformation is startling. Any trace of the man behind the beast is gone. The creature that stands before me is pure Migoi. He throws his head back and roars, "Run!"

Fear slams into my stomach like a lead weight, dragging at my limbs until instinct kicks in, screaming at me to do just that. I spin and bolt, darting into the nearest tunnel. I have no idea where I am going, I don't think, just keep moving, feet pounding against the uneven ground as though the devil himself is chasing me.

My feet slip over the loose rocks in the dark passages, but I push myself, muscles burning, lungs bursting as I run faster than I ever thought possible. My steps falter as I'm faced with a split. The left tunnel seems to head up, and I feel a breeze from it, so I choose that direction.

My calves sting with the added exertion of the incline, but I keep running. I burst forth into a cave that has somehow captured the night sky. I stare in wonder at the tiny bursts of light all around me.

As I look around the cave, I see it is full of glittering crystals, reflecting the light back at me through their facets. The beautiful distraction is my downfall. Air whooshes out of my lungs as a strong arm wraps around my middle and snatches me from where I stand. A startled scream leaves my lips before a hand clamps down over my mouth.

Harsh panting in my ear turns to wicked laughter as he growls out, "Mine."

I sink my teeth into the fleshy palm covering my mouth, startling him enough to drop me. I take off back the way I came, feeling smug at my escape until a hand wraps itself in my hair streaming behind me. I'm brought up short, pain prickling delightfully across my scalp as fear pools in my belly.

Pressure on my head forces me to my knees, the harsh ground biting into my flesh. I can't help but cry out as a pebble lodges into my knee. A shove to my back has me falling forward, catching myself on my palms.

A hiss escapes my mouth as he curls his massive form over me, trapping me between his large body and the cool earth. A satisfied growl rumbles from his chest as he subdues his prey.

I had longed for this, to be taken by him in his full Yeti form in a pure primal claiming, but now that I'm trapped, I'm not so sure. Before I can think it through, my body reacts—bucking wildly, trying to throw him off, but it's futile. I can't so much as budge the creature wrapped around me.

He brings his nose to my hair, scenting me. As his breath cascades over my ear and neck, shivers race down my spine, leaving goosebumps in their wake. I turn my head, desperate to catch a glimpse of those luminous eyes I love so much. Instead, I am rewarded with a snarl and a lick up the side of my face.

One large hand palms the back of my head, forcing it down to the ground while the other wrenches my hips up higher into the air. Great, snuffling breaths trace down my spine and over my ass. I hear a sharp inhale followed by a satisfied moan, my only warning before he begins to feast on me from behind.

He laps at my pussy, my ass, my cheeks, devouring me. The building sensations are a direct counterpoint to the harsh earth digging into my hands and knees. My head and body are pinned, immobile. All I can do is pant through the rush of being eaten by a starving creature. His great tongue probes at my entrance, slipping inside of me.

A moan escapes my lips at the sensation of being filled with his wet, muscular, thrusting tongue. In his full Yeti form, its so large it feels like being fucked by a man. Within seconds, my hips are trying to grind back into it, but I'm pinned. When he pulls it out, a plea falls from my mouth.

"Oh, please," I beg, wanting the warm heat to return to my dripping core. "Please."

"Please what?" he snarls.

"Please, do that again," I whimper.

"Do what?" he demands, voice rough.

My cheeks flame at having to say it out loud, but my clenching core aches to be filled. "Please put your tongue inside me again."

A dark chuckle precedes his return, but instead of slipping his large tongue back into my sex, he spears it directly into my ass. A startled scream morphs into a long continuous moan at the decadent sensation of the wet, pulsating warmth inside my forbidden hole.

A large finger probes at my pussy, and the sensation of being completely filled has pleasure spiraling through me. I feel my core begin to clench rhythmically at his finger when he abruptly pulls out.

"No," I cry out, only to feel two large fingers return to my entrance. I hiss at the stretch as he scissors and twists them inside of me. Slowly the pressure bleeds into pleasure. As my moans pick up, I feel a third finger fighting to slip in with the others.

The stretch is almost unbearable until his tongue is again probing at my ass. As it slips inside, I marvel at the glorious pressure. Never did I imagine I could fit such a volume into my pussy but I had always dreamed of being filled and stretched just like this.

My moans and cries turn into one long incomprehensible torrent as I am overwhelmed by the sensations and pleasure coiling in my belly. He thrusts his fingers and tongue in unison, the thin membrane separating them becoming more sensitized.

He explores every inch of skin inside of me and zeroes in on the exact rhythm and spots that have me begging for more. The sounds of my desire and cries of pleasure echo around us in the cave.

The pressure builds and builds into a crescendo, and I cry out, screaming as I feel fluid drench my thighs, gushing out past the fullness of his fingers. While I am still gripped by the aftershocks of the intense orgasm, he pulls his hands and mouth away, grips my hips, and lines up his massive cock at my entrance.

Finally, the moment I've been waiting for. This is what I wanted. Craved. Hungered for him to mate me in his full Yeti form, no holding back. I spread my knees wider and brace myself on my arms to prepare for the onslaught, thankful he has tried to ready me.

But nothing could have prepared me to take the cock of an eight foot Yeti in rut.

The large tapered head pushes against my opening, pulsing with heat. His hands hold my hips steady as he enters me, his harsh breaths filling the air as he fights to breach my opening. By some miracle my body opens to him, allowing him to slowly sink his monster cock inside me.

It feels twice as large as the last time. Thicker. Longer. Every pulsating vein, every ridge is an exquisite texture sliding over my sensitized nerve endings. My own harsh pants echo in my ears.

He bottoms out against my cervix, but I know I still haven't taken all of him. He wraps his arms around my body and holds me suspended in front of him, managing to caress my breasts with one hand while the other applies pressure to my belly and clit.

All I can do is lie there, taking his cock as he pushes in a little further after every retreat. I feel my stomach moving with each thrust, and pleasure begins to swell within me. His shaggy soft hair envelops me, his body curled around mine. Pure animalistic pleasure.

I imagine what we must look like, a great beast rutting into a helpless female, and the taboo thought pushes me further into dark decadence. On and on he thrusts, my body goes limp from exhaustion, every muscle shaking, but still he fucks into me, his hips picking up the pace, faster and faster.

Everything blurs into sensation and heat. I can feel him

warm even more around me and within me, the large veins that line his impressive cock pulsing. Sweat drips off my body just as my arousal drips down my thighs. Time has lost all meaning, the only thing that exists now is pleasure and heat.

He withdraws only long enough to flip me onto my back. Sliding one hand under my head and one under my hips, he angles my body and drives into me deeper than ever. Each long thrust drags against every nerve ending that is on fire. Each slam of his hips into mine rubs his thick textured curls over my clit in a delicious counter point.

I try to wrap my legs around him, desperate for more, but can barely get them around his body. The caves echo with our shared cries until I feel him growing impossibly larger at his base where we are connected.

I think—is he knotting us together?

His breathing turns harsh, and he buries his face into the juncture of my neck and shoulder. A low growl starts, vibrating from his chest against my skin. It picks up in volume until his whole body is consumed with it, vibrating against me.

I tilt my hips, trying to get more of the delicious sensation directly against my sensitive bundle of nerves. The knot grows and grows, and just when I think it will split me in two, he roars his release and sinks his teeth into my neck.

Great, thick jets of hot cum spurt into me, bathing my insides in scalding heat. I scream with him, my voice hoarse, body convulsing as my own release wracks through me at the sensation of being filled with liquid fire.

His movements finally still, but his knot remains firmly inside of me, holding his release within. He wraps his arms around my waist and rolls to his back, carrying me with him. I burrow into his fur and warmth, filled with his seed and sealed with his knot.

I try to shift my hips but find we are fused together, which suits me just fine. There is nowhere else I would rather be, than right here with him.

"Eryon," I whisper into his velvet skin, my voice raspy from screaming.

"Mhm," he mumbles in reply.

"The tea you gave me—," I start, but he lays his finger across my lips, silencing my question before I can voice it.

"I knew you were my mate from the first time I saw you looking for the plant. The way you were bent over, that sweet ass on display for me," he quips as he grabs a double handful of that same body part and chuckles.

Voice turning serious he says, "Then the sun lit up your hair like the most beautiful sunset I've ever seen in all my long years of existence, and all I could think about was sinking my hands deep into your curls and sliding my cock between your lips."

I feel him begin to lengthen again inside of me, my insides turning molten as he slowly slides his hands up from ass to bury them deep in my hair. Tilting my head up to meet my eyes, his voice turns soft but insistent.

"But when I saw your eyes, shimmering like the winter star itself in the moonlight, I knew you were a gift from the gods of creation, and I loved you from that moment. The flower was always meant to be yours, Sruhnar."

He begins to slowly thrust inside of me again, reflecting the intensity of his words as he continues. "So yes, I hid it in your bag even when it broke my heart to send you away."

Another powerful stroke fills me, pulling a gasp from my lips as he declares, "I was a fool. A hurt one, but a fool nonetheless. So, when you swept back into my life like the north winds and then tried to sacrifice yourself for me, you're damn right I poured its healing elixir down your throat."

His hips pick up a punishing pace as he stares deep into my soul. He gives a small shake of my head as his hands tremble with intensity. Each declaration punctuated with a thrust, he vows, "I will never, never, be separated from you again. You are my mate, Sruhnar, my winter star, and nothing, not even death, can take you from me."

I detonate around him, overflowing with his love and the intensity of knowing—I love him just as fiercely.

Welcome to Yeti Season. Feral, fluffy, & fiercely devoted. Ready for more?

If you're not ready to be done with *Yeti or Knot*, neither was I. This story began as a novella, but I fell so deeply in love with Dahlia, Eryon, and their world that I immediately expanded it into a full-length novel. *Winter Star* features over 50,000 words of additional content, including dual POV, expanded worldbuilding, and a bonus epilogue you won't want to miss. You can continue their journey here: https://a.co/d/dMYKRwJ

For more cinnamon roll cryptid chaos, don't miss *Chosen by the Yeti*—new heroine, new world, same swoony Yeti monster energy.
Can you find the link between these worlds?
Continue Yeti season here:
https://a.co/d/eL0D0Qk

Acknowledgments

Thank you to my emotional support editing team Beth Hudson, Ink, my PA and all around champion Amanda, my alpha & beta teams (Amanda, Bree, Nicole, Lauren, Lianne), my ARC & street teams, and the monster queen herself, Biblio Barbie, for all of her support and encouragement. To my family and friends, thank you for your love and patience as I talked about Yetis for months.

Thank *you*, my darling readers, for getting lost in the frost with me.

And finally, thank you to my mother for my love of reading. I put a piece of her into every story I write, that she may live on forever.

Follow me @CassandraElizzabeth and visit cassandraelizzabeth.com to subscribe to my newsletter, get updates on upcoming books, and join my reader community.

If you enjoyed this story, please consider leaving a review—it means everything to indie authors.

Namaste,

Cassandra

ABOUT THE AUTHOR

Cassandra Elizzabeth writes love stories that bleed—dark romance, monsters, and heroines who don't just survive, but rewrite the stories meant to destroy them. Her work blends gothic atmosphere, raw emotion, and the dangerous beauty of love that refuses to die.

She is the author of the *Immortal Redemption* series and several upcoming monster romances. Cassandra proudly identifies as a disabled and rare disease author. As a gene carrier for a fully penetrant form of a terminal disease, she writes on borrowed time—and makes every word count.

Through her stories, she explores legacy, longing, obsession, and the defiant hope that even the darkest love can still heal. When she's not writing, she's chasing her twins, fighting for rare disease awareness, or tending her garden full of strange and beautiful flowers—always searching for the ones that bloom in the dark.